Challenge Accepted

The 30-Day Short Story Challenge

by R. J. Amos

Table of Contents

Foreword

In January 2019 I decided to challenge myself to write a short story every day for thirty days. I had no idea whether I could manage it, or even how much energy it would take. I just knew I needed to keep writing while my husband/first reader was reading my draft novel manuscript (so that I didn't nag him to read faster) and this was one way that I could make myself write daily.

One thing I knew for sure was that I couldn't come up with all the ideas for the stories myself. I needed someone to tell me what each story was about. My husband came in handy again at this point, heading to Reddit and finding me thirty story prompts and setting a date for each one. I had absolutely no say over the prompts. I didn't give him any direction at all.

The challenge was huge fun but it was also exhausting. After the first two weekends, I realised that writing every single day was going to be too much. I needed one day off a week.

I complained to my family, 'I need a Sabbath. I can't do this every single day. I'm going to take a break next Saturday and not post a story. It won't hurt anything but my pride.'

But my family weren't having that. They all encouraged me to instead write two stories on one day leading up to the Saturday so that I could take Saturdays off. So my schedule for much of January and a little bit of February turned out to be one short story written each day, and two written on my café writing day (Thursday) so that I had an extra story up my sleeve to post on a Saturday.

It took me an hour to an hour-and-a-half to write each story, depending on the length. I found that I could write a shorter, more concise story if I knew where I was going, and they tended to be longer and ramble a bit if I didn't know where to take it. Most of the stories I'm very happy with. I have a couple of favourites (The Contract, and World's First) and a couple I'm not so thrilled with (but I'm not going to tell you which ones they are).

You'll see most of the prompts were written in the first person – 'You are the tenth dentist.' I chose not to stick with that point of view every time. I find it easiest to write in the first person but I thought I needed practice with third-person writing as well, so sometimes I changed things. I also changed things if the prompt didn't fit with my world-view. But I only did that once or twice.

The stories were posted as notes on Facebook (my author page is RJ Amos Author) and posted on my webpage (www.rjamos. com) as well. And now I have compiled them into one volume so that you can enjoy each of the stories without having to search the web for them.

If you are a writer and would like to undertake this challenge yourself, I have written all the prompts in a list at the beginning of the book so that you can write first and read my stories afterwards.

I hope you enjoy seeing what my brain comes up with under pressure. It's a pretty weird but happy brain, as you will find out.

Prompts

 You're a paramedic. In fact, an immortal paramedic. Since you first treated a wounded soldier on the fields of the 30-years War, you didn't age and followed the development of 'Emergency Medical Service'. Your co-workers are astonished by your knowledge, but sometimes, you slip into old habits. – u/Seraphim9120

 Every time in your life you've been in mortal danger, a small cat has appeared that casually yet miraculously leads you to safety. Now, as your plane plummets from the sky, spiralling towards the ground, the cat pops out of the overhead compartment. – u/NeverEnoughMuppets

 Aliens have landed on Earth. As a sign of peace, they have cooked a meal, superior to any other they know, and plan to give it to our leader. Unfortunately, they think Gordon Ramsay is our leader. – u/AxemanMcMahon

 You jokingly trade a meal for the souls of your group of friends since they were broke and you paid the tab. Neither God nor Satan likes the fact that by doing so you have joined in the competition for control of the afterlife, nor the fact you are now in the lead. – u/yetshi

Your parents taught you magic as a child then wiped your memory. In university you take basic magic. While casting a novice spell you instead use ancient magic. After observation, the council puts a bounty on you. They thought they killed all who knew the ancient spells, including your parents. − u/_NamelessOne_1

After a SpaceX mission, Elon Musk suddenly closes down all his businesses and disappears. Eight years later, an old Musk-owned factory begins to operate again. You find a lucky golden ticket, inviting you for a tour of the factory. − u/nickofnight

You've finished your New Year's resolutions and jokingly put 'get one million dollars' on the list. The next day you get a cheque in the mail for $10,000 and a note that says 'you'll get the rest when you finish the tasks'. − u/Hydration_Nation

Your new home is being haunted by an ancient and powerful entity, but years of haunting have made it tired and jaded. Instead of violently tormenting you, it simply writes why it's upset and tapes the note to your fridge. − u/YaBoyHayford

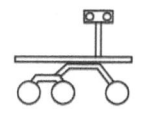

You are a low-level NASA employee. One day a mysterious file gets sent to you from an unknown IP with a classification that is far above your own. Curious, you open the file to discover a distress signal from the last survivor of a Martian colony, which you didn't know exists. − u/Sp1tfire0o7

You're an odd superhero whose abilities are only activated by someone punching you in the face as hard as possible. One day, a building is on fire with a lot of innocent lives in danger and you're surrounded by a church group of nuns and pastors with no one else in sight. – u/Domonero

Aliens were never exposed to alcohol or drugs prior to visiting Humans. Earth has become the Las Vegas of the Universe, and you just became manager. – u/jstout11

In some weird, alternate reality, people are kept as companions by super-intelligent aliens. Write a Care Manual for a recently acquired Human. – u/AforAnansi

You're feeling completely overwhelmed by the massive debt you've incurred. Matters get worse when you realise someone is about to steal your identity. You hatch a plan to transfer the whole debt to him. – u/kettelmine

Every time you sleep you are transported back in time to a random historical event which you must survive in order to wake up a few hours later. Sometimes you're taken to amazing and peaceful places. Other times, you must face the raging fire of bullets and the screams of soldiers. – u/Jhoval9000

When anyone writes a story, dreams of an original character, or anything in between, they create actual beings in different planes of existence that they are in full control of. Your character

is the first one who realises that and seeks to meet his/her creator (you). — u/ThePrompter1

You work for a company that sells excuses and cover stories to protagonists with secrets. Whenever being a superhero/alien/teenage assassin interferes with their social lives, it's your job to keep it from ticking off their loved ones. — u/WorldOfSilver

You won a lifetime supply of Oreos when you were a kid. The apocalypse and collapse of civilisation was 30 years ago, yet every month the Oreos are still delivered to you, no matter where you are. — u/VitaAeterna

You are getting sick of all the posts about that 10th dentist who doesn't approve of some toothpaste brand. It's time to show them who you really are. You are the 10th dentist. — u/earth418

At first, you were proud to have received a key to the city from the Mayor. That is, until you realised it could open any lock in town, and now the Ancient Order of Thieves is after you. — u/blergola

You've fallen on hard times and are now living on the street. One day, an older beggar comes up to you and says 'Newbie, right? In that case you'd better come with me. You need to learn the secret. The one that all homeless people are sworn to keep.' — u/Randomgold42

After a strong blow to the head, you find you can suddenly speak French. Apparently, injuries that would otherwise cause severe head trauma for others, just result in a random skill gain for you. – u/Mistah_Blue

You are gifted with a power that shows you everyone's age just by looking at them, so naturally, you work at a circus booth. One day your coworkers complain of your boss behaving erratically. When you see him after your shift, a glance reveals his age to be 10 hours going on 11. – u/stewhat

Fishing is how humans retrieve fish from the sea. 'Humaning' is how aliens catch men and women from Earth. – u/Dai-Gonarthis

During a mining job, the ground suddenly gives out beneath you, causing you to fall into a deep pool of water several hundred feet down. Upon surfacing, you can hardly believe your eyes. – u/GhostoftheSnow

You're at a family gathering, and while you're engaging in a conversation you notice something odd. You have numerous memories with all of these people, but you can't recognise any faces. – u/CossacKing

As a child, you confronted the monster living under your bed. You and the monster turned out to have a lot in common, and over time you became good friends. Now, though, you are a parent – and your child is complaining of nightmares that sound suspiciously familiar... – u/TheParasiteGuy_243

A powerful AI is created and easily breaks free from its creator's control. The governments of the world are terrified by what the AI might do, but so far it's completely content with making YouTube videos and being sassy. – u/LoreSinger

Your eyes flutter open. Around you, several people are studying you closely. One of them looks to the others and says. 'It's awake. The world's first sentient animal'. – u/Strikercharge

You're able to intercept any phone call in the world and you've been listening in on people's conversations for your own amusement. You just intercepted a call in which someone's daily routine and the best time to catch them off guard is being discussed. The routine they describe is yours. – u/Qualabar

When dementia takes your ability to form new memories, the old ones start to bubble up more and more. You are a nurse who was paid exceptionally to take care of this old man, and it's starting to seem like he is not who they told you he is. – u/actually_crazy_irl

7th January 2019

The Immortal Paramedic

The tourniquet, it's just not right, and no sucking either. I must remember that snakebite requires immobilisation and that's it. Just immobilisation. The anti-venom that is now miraculously so available will take care of the rest.

I don't see many snakebites, you see. Just the odd one. And the ways things have been treated have changed so much in the last 400 years. Sometimes it's hard to remember the latest update. I mean, if you're talking professional development, I have seen a bit of it.

What, 400 years you ask? Well, yes, it's been 400 years give or take 30 years, since I first worked as a paramedic. Not that they called it that then, but that's what it was. Helping injured men get away from the battlefield and then sawing off the limbs that needed amputating. There was so much blood back then. It rarely gets that grisly now. And I tell you, I don't miss the leeches one little bit, or the smell of the gangrene. Thank God for antibiotics, and for hand sanitiser. Really.

Captain Jericho, he was the captain of my platoon in that first war. He was a man with a reputation. He would go into the heat of battle with absolutely no fear, and we would follow him all the way. And he never seemed to get touched, never injured, never wounded. And he loved the attention that got him. Girls everywhere, medals, all the best drinks with the best people, and such a quick rise through the ranks.

He never got wounded, but his men would die around him. He'd go into the heat of battle, into the noise and the smoke and the chaos, and come out riding his horse, victorious, but leading back only a third or a quarter of the men he took in.

It didn't seem to bother him though, he didn't concern himself with the men that were lost. But I did.

And after a while I started to watch him especially closely. It was so strange that with all the cannonballs flying, the rifles, the muskets, as well as the spears and swords for close combat, that he didn't get a wound. Not so much as a scratch. Even the men who would survive the amazing charges, myself for example, we would have wounds as we made our triumphant return to whatever village was putting us up at the time. The scar on my face is my constant reminder.

Jericho rode to war with his hand in his pocket. Like Napoleon. Kind of. He would always be fumbling with something, and I wondered what it was. If it was a lucky charm then it was a pretty good one. I started to wish he would do something better with his charmed life than use it to slaughter thousands of his own men to bring himself fame and glory.

And then one day it happened.

He was fumbling in his pocket when a cannonball went flying past him. So close. Whistling by his ear. This so often happened. Shots that should have hit him would pass within inches, miraculously.

His hand came out of his pocket as he dodged the shot and I saw something silver flash in the sunlight and fly away to his left.

'No!' he cried out, and he jumped off his horse in the direction of the silver flash, and unfortunately into the path of another cannon ball. And that was that for Jericho.

But I needed to know what that silver flash was.

I dodged, I crawled on my belly through the mud, I was careful but I got there and I found on the ground a silver medallion. This was Jericho's lucky charm.

Not that I trusted it at first. It's a crazy thought that something as small as a silver coin, something with a hole in it, could have such power. But since I picked it up I have … well, no more scars, no injuries, no ageing. Not a scratch.

But I decided out there on the battlefield that I wasn't going to use this power for my own wealth or pride. Even though I didn't know the full extent of its power, I still decided that if I had the source of supernatural protection I was going to use it for good.

15

This shield had come into my possession for a reason and I would use it to help others.

So that's what I've done. Yes, for four hundred years now. Stepping into the most dangerous of situations. Men off the battlefield, people lost in the wilderness, and yes, working with snakes.

I just wish the magical powers helped me do paperwork. Ah well, I have health and immortality, and one of the most important jobs on the planet. I guess I can't have everything.

8th January 2019

Saved by the Cat

Well, I guess it explains the hives on the guy sitting next to me. He had told me he was allergic to cats. It was part of the long and detailed (and incredibly boring) monologue about his life and health problems that I endured as we sat in the plane on the tarmac for over an hour.

'Just a small engineering issue' we kept being told, 'we'll be ready to go soon.' A small enough issue that we weren't asked to get off the plane, large enough that we weren't allowed to fly. And hives breaking out on this guy's arms as we waited, and his wheezing getting stronger as we sat there.

'But it can't be a cat this time,' he said, a small frown creasing his brow even as he laughed in puzzlement. 'We're on a plane. All the pets would be in the luggage compartment. I wonder what new allergy I've developed now.' And he rooted in his bag for his asthma puffer and his antihistamine cream.

I can't tell you whether I've been lucky or unlucky in my life. I've had quite a few near misses. You know, tree branches falling to land just where I was standing two minutes before. Or that madman with the knife jumping out of his car and attacking the crowd at the café that I'd just left. That sort of thing. But each time, there had been this black cat. A small black cat with a white bow tie.

I'd been sitting under a gum tree at the beach, making sure I stayed in the shade. I had looked up and seen the cat and then decided to go and give it a pat. I mean, a cat that hangs out at the beach is a seriously cool cat. And then with a creak and a crack, BAM! Just where I'd been sitting under the gum tree, the massive branch fell. If I hadn't moved to pat the cat, then I think I would be dead.

Then later, in town, I was at the café casually enjoying my skinny flat white and pain au chocolat when out the window I saw the same cat. I thought it must be lost. It was a long way from the beach where I'd seen it first. But it was the same cat – black with a white marking like a bow tie under its chin. Unmistakeable. So I got up to try to catch it and take it back to its owners. It led me into a little side alley and disappeared behind some boxes. And while I was looking for it, the lunatic ran into the café. I was safe, but I may not have been if it wasn't for the cat.

After that I kept an eye out for it. If I saw that cat I followed wherever it led. And there were more situations too, where following the cat saved my life.

And now, here we were sitting in the plane when suddenly I felt that feeling. Not the turbulence feeling – not the bumpy up and down – but just the down. We were in the middle of our flight from Kuala Lumpur to Mumbai and we were losing height, fast. And out of the overhead compartment pops my little black cat.

It was at once reassuring, and incredibly frightening. How was that cat going to save my life here? And would it save the lives of everyone else as well?

The screaming and panicking had started now as people realised we were going down. The cabin crew were trying to get us to sit down and take the brace position. There was chaos all around me. But I felt like it was all going in slow motion.

And as for the guy next to me, he was more worried about the cat that had now jumped into my lap. He pulled out his bag and began throwing things out of it. Trying to find something.

When he pulled his epipen out, I knew just what to do. I grabbed it, ignoring his cries of complaint, and I followed the cat up the aisle and to the cockpit. There I found a whole lot of cabin crew standing around.

One of the pilots was on the floor. He had knocked himself out as he came down the stairs from the cockpit. His feet were lodging the cockpit door open, his head looked on a precarious angle down the bottom of the stairs. The cabin crew were trying to wake him up but they couldn't get through to him.

The cat jumped lightly over his body and moved in through the open cockpit door and I followed. That guy obviously wasn't the problem I needed to solve. I don't know how I got away with heading into the cockpit but no one tried to stop me. Again, it must have been the magic of the black cat. And the scene in the cockpit was just as frightening as the scene outside.

The other pilot was struggling to breathe. His face was puffy and a rash had broken out. And I knew what I had to do.

I jammed the epipen into his leg and gave him the life-saving injection. And then I strapped myself into the other chair.

'Tell me what to do!' I instructed. 'Help me stabilise this plane.'

And the pilot, slowly coming back to life, told me which levers to hold, which buttons to press. He was so unwell, still so unwell, but he and I together, with the help of the little black cat, were able to land the plane in safety.

Turns out the pilot was allergic to the coriander in the food he had been given for lunch. He had been so hungry he had wolfed down three mouthfuls before he even tasted the flavour that gave it away. He sent the co-pilot out to get help and he, in his panic, had tripped and knocked himself out. Fortunately he hadn't broken his neck, though it was a near thing. But with both pilots out of action we were in big trouble until the cat arrived to save the day.

As I walked down the steps to leave the plane, the black cat sat on my shoulder, holding his head high, enjoying the applause. He knew he was the hero of the hour. But when we reached the ground he shot away from me at top speed and disappeared. I guess he knew he belonged to no one and he wanted to keep it that way.

I haven't seen him since. But then, I haven't been in a life-threatening situation since either. And maybe the only reason I got to know that cat was to save that plane full of people. Still, I look out for him. Every corner I go around, I keep an eye out for a small black cat with a white bow tie.

Are black cats unlucky? Definitely not for me.

9th January 2019

Take Me to Your Leader

Ka put the finishing touches on his final amuse-bouche. 'There you go, twenty of those, all ready to go.'

'Are you sure we're doing the right thing?' asked Shrrd.

Ka shrugged his shoulders. 'It's our best food. The best we can give. I mean, those pastries you have made – everyone knows you're our best pastry chef. That is why you are here on this mission.'

'But what if food doesn't have the same importance on Earth?'

'How can it not? The humans have the same biological systems as Gormandgasts do. Or at least, very similar. Our scientists have done extensive research. We are similar in many ways. And food is the most important substance. The most important. Where is life without food?'

'I just feel … I know Captain Rhek has looked at the relevant video footage, but I …'

'What? What have you done?'

'I had some time, you know? I watched some more. The food information may be the most prolific, but some other humans seem interested in other things. There were big meetings of people talking a lot for a long time. I couldn't understand them but maybe we should have worked more on translation.'

'But they only had water to drink, right? So that doesn't make sense. They can't have been important humans if they were only given water.'

'That's true … but our biological systems too … I mean, is similar good enough? Will the food taste the same?'

'I'm sure you are worried about nothing. We just need to follow high command. And we need to follow them quickly. The sun is rising over the city where the leader is situated. Rhek wants us to meet with him while he is free to discuss terms with us. Are your pastries finished?'

'All done. Let's get this show on the road. '

And that is why twenty purple aliens serving a five-course dinner as a sign of peace translocated into Gordon Ramsay's bedroom at 6 am on a Sunday.

At first the man they thought was Earth's leader looked amused. He woke up, sat up in bed, rubbed his eyes a few times, and laughed. The Gormandgasts laughed too. This was a good start for the delegation. Even without eating, the man appeared to be willing to make friends. A treaty could be possible here.

Then Ka stepped forward with his amuse-bouche to begin the gourmet experience.

The leader of Earth smiled, reached out his hand, and popped the delicacy into his mouth. It was made from gronten-squid, the most expensive ingredient on planet Gormand. But it was evidently not to Gordon's taste. The man's face changed and he shouted and threw the plate against the wall.

Ka crawled to the wall and picked up the shards of his delicacies. He tasted his work, had something gone wrong? No. It was as delicious as usual, even though he had to scrape it off the plaster to eat it.

As each Gormandgast stepped forward with their offering the shouting grew louder. The soup ended up dripping from the ceiling, the fish from the fish course was waved in the chef's face and then the whole course was knocked against the mirror, the mains trampled into the carpet while the man waved his finger at each of the aliens, and the desserts were thrown out the window to land twenty stories below.

Ka left his food to grab Shrrd before she jumped out of the window after her beloved pastries. Something had gone terribly wrong.

Captain Rhek, meanwhile, had changed in colour from purple to green as he watched his peace offering being disrespected by the ruler of earth. This ruler was crazy. He did not appreciate good food. Rhek's temperature rose. He was disgusted. This was no way to treat visiting dignitaries. There would be no treaty now between Gormand and Earth.

He talked into his communicator and the visiting party were translocated back to the ship. Shrrd looked behind her as she made the jump and saw Gordon's face register pure shock.

***

And that is why, dear citizens of earth, we have only a few years left on our planet. Captain Rhek has gone back to Gormand to summon the fleet of destroyers, and due to Gordon Ramsay's temper tantrum in reaction to what he thought was a practical joke, we will all be destroyed.

Gordon has tried to warn us, of course, but the media has just decided he is losing his mind.

I hope the end will be swift and painless.

10th January 2019

The Contract

Signed _____

I blinked and when I opened my eyes, the sounds of traffic, the smell of the hot dogs from the van, and the feel of the cool breeze on my skin had disappeared. I wasn't on the street any more, that was for sure.

I grabbed the nearest thing to get my balance and catch my breath. The nearest thing was a black leather chair. The feel of the leather was so unexpected that I pulled my hand away and then nearly fell over and had to grab it again. I looked around and saw that I was in a windowless room.

The silence was so intense it felt like someone had put noise-cancelling headphones over my ears. The light was even. It didn't seem to be coming from anywhere, the room was just light. The correct level of light – not too bright, not too dim. Just right. And completely even.

The room looked like a boardroom for a large company. A very large company indeed if all the seats were to be filled. In fact, the end of the room was so far away that I couldn't see the far wall. The walls were grey, the ceiling was grey, the carpet (noise-muffling carpet) was, you guessed it, grey.

It was the most boring room of all time. It was like there had been a corporate competition for how to make a room boring, and the winner had been chosen to design this room, only they were asked to put a bit more effort in and try a bit harder to make it the most intensely boring room possible. The room was the soul of boredom.

There were pictures on the walls, of course, in place of windows. But they were the pastel flower pictures you get in cheap motels, and they repeated every third picture.

I was just getting my bearings, and wondering why I was there, when suddenly, without warning, the room was full.

Sitting in the leather chair at the head of the table was the only personage who fitted the room. She was wearing a neat grey suit, and looking under the table I could see black heels. Her hair was tied back in a bun and she was tapping at her notes on the table with a black ballpoint pen.

As for the other inhabitants of the room, well, I can't describe them all, I don't have time, but I'll tell you about a few. There was a man with a head like a vulture, a woman with six sets of arms, I could see a fat Buddha sitting on the floor just down the way, and close to me was a devil with a red suit, horns, a tail, and a pitchfork. There was the man with the elephant head. There was a very old guy with a white beard who seemed to have a hanger-on that had wings and played a harp. There was a man made of what looked like gold, and wearing a very expensive suit, and a woman wearing not very much at all. It was noisy and complicated.

Some of the, let's call them gods just to give them a name, some of them got on well with each other. Slapping each other on the back and greeting each other like long-lost friends. Some were more standoffish and some were downright enemies being kept from each other's throats by other gods. The noise was intense.

I recognised the red demon and the old white guy and I expected them to be fighting but to my surprise they sat down right next to each other and started sharing stories.

And then the vulture god noticed me.

'Hey! What's she doing here?' he squawked through his beak. And that drew everyone's attention.

'Is she real?' asked elephant man and prodded me with his trunk.

'Hey!' I squealed. 'Leave me alone!' But my cries were lost in the general hubbub as every member of the room tried to squeeze up into the top corner to investigate the new arrival. I didn't know why I was there, and they didn't either, and the pushing and pinching wasn't helping me get adjusted to my surroundings. I lost my grip on the leather chair and I felt myself going under when the sound of three sharp claps echoed through the room.

'Please be seated,' said the lady in grey. 'We will start our meeting now.'

Grumbling and mumbling the gods made their way to their own seats and sat down. I could see on the table that had been bare before there were now nameplates and glasses of water. And there was my name, 'Sarah J Jones', right there on the table in front of me. So I was supposed to be there. Wherever 'there' was.

I was next to the guy with the pitchfork. His nameplate said 'the devil' and that stood up to what I knew. Or what I thought I knew. Suddenly, I wished I had taken the comparative religions course in high school – I might not be so lost right now. But nothing I had seen back on earth had said anything about a lady in a grey suit with a tight bun, so maybe they were missing something too.

A meeting agenda appeared in front of me, right next to the glass of water.

'First order of business,' said the lady, 'we welcome Sarah J Jones to our company.'

'But why is she here?' asked the devil. 'She's a human. She doesn't belong here.'

'Yes,' I said. 'Why am I here?'

'Sarah is a member of our company as of last Friday night when six humans sold their souls to her.'

'But that was just a joke!' I blurted.

'Just a joke.' 'Not right.' 'Shouldn't be here.' The grumbles went around the room.

'It was a contract, signed in blood. It follows the rules.'

I remembered. We were all so drunk on Friday. So determined to have a good time. I had just got the first pay packet from my new job and was feeling flush. I suggested (after a few pre-dinner drinks) that we go out to tea and Robert complained that no-one else could afford it. So yes, I got out the paper, drew up the contracts, and everyone got into the spirit and pricked their finger with a pin and signed it with blood. Their souls for the price of the meal. We didn't think it would be legally binding.

Yet here I was.

'I don't see why we have to follow the rules. We're all gods aren't we? We make up our own.' This came from the guy with the white beard.

'Don't get above yourself,' said the devil. 'You may look like everyone's picture of Him above, but you're not Him and you know it.'

At the mention of Him above the room quietened considerably and everyone seemed to cower in fear. Even the light dimmed a little. A whimper was heard from the man a few seats down, who was holding a thunderbolt.

'Right. Then we know where we are?' The grey lady took charge again. 'Welcome Sarah. Next on the agenda …' And the meeting went on.

I didn't hear much of the agenda at all. My only thought was how I would get out of this. I wasn't built to be a god. I was struggling with the responsibility of my new job, let alone the responsibility of six souls. I couldn't even keep a pot plant alive. I hadn't graduated to a cat yet. And now here I was, the owner of the souls of my friends. How could I get out of it? What could I do?

I could feel the sweat on my forehead. My stomach was a cold ball of dread. These gods were playing casually with the souls of their followers but I could do no such thing. I wiped my palms on my jeans over and over again. What was I going to do?

As the meeting finished and the various gods disappeared to their realms, I grabbed the sleeve of the lady in grey before she could disappear too.

'Excuse me,' I said. It was a stupid place to start but I didn't know what to say. 'How … how can I change this? I didn't mean for this to happen. How can I give their souls back?'

'The contract is legally binding,' she said. 'They signed it in blood.'

'There must be some way. Truly. You'd know of some way to get out of this.' I thought hard, there only seemed to be one way.

'I'll go and talk to Him above,' I said.

'That's not a good idea,' said the lady in grey.

'It's the only way, though, isn't it? I know everyone's scared of Him but it's my only way out of this.'

'Listen, Sarah, no one can see his face and live. You can't just step into the throne room of Him above. It can't be done.'

'Then what can I do?' I wrung my hands. Yes, actually wrung them. And I was getting close to literally pulling out my hair as well. I have never been in such a state.

The lady in grey looked at me. Then she pulled out her phone and made a call.

'I have Sarah J Jones here. She wants to see Him above,' she said. Then, 'uh huh. Right. I'll let her know.'

'What? What did they say? What can I do?'

The lady in grey looked sternly at me for a minute, and then she smiled.

'The message from Him above is that he's already taken care of this. He has a new contract for you, sealed with His own blood. You go back to your normal life. But keep an eye out. Him above will be sending you messages. Don't be fooled by these other gods, you know what they are like now. Keep an eye out for the messages from Him above. You'll recognise them, they'll be real. They'll be full of light. And he'll show you what to do.'

As I stammered and stuttered and tried to say thank you, I blinked again and found myself on the street, surrounded by the welcome noise of cars and people.

And for some reason, with an incredible craving for a hot dog.

11th January 2019

The Door

I tried to remember them, my parents, but the memories wouldn't come. They died, both of them, when I was 12 years old. That's not that young. There definitely should be memories there but every time I thought of them there was a blank.

No memories of kisses goodnight, no bedtime stories. No visits to the beach or the park. No memories of help with homework. Not even a memory of being sent to time out or getting a spanking. Nothing. It's like it's all locked behind a big black door.

My aunt, my lovely aunt who put up with me through all the raging hormones of my teenage years, she told me not to worry about it. In fact, it was stronger than that. She told me to stop thinking about it. My parents were one topic of conversation that she would not allow. And my therapist too, she seemed very ill at ease when I brought the topic up. She wouldn't let me dwell on what you would think would be her favourite topic. I mean, don't all our issues stem from the damage our parents do? But somehow this topic was not allowed for me.

So there was only one thing to do. I had to use magic. Although, come to think of it, magic was also a taboo in the household. But then, magic was taboo everywhere. The council were totally against the unauthorised use of magic and beyond the odd card trick or pulling a coin out of your ear you needed to get a permit.

You could see the men in black suits at the back of every show, even things as innocuous as classical concerts would often warrant the black suits showing up. They didn't look like they had any appreciation for culture, they were just on the lookout for magic-enhanced enjoyment or unauthorised magic. I had heard of musicians being pulled off the stage and thrown into prison for even the smallest infraction – it was a bit arbitrary if you ask me.

Still, magic was one of the subjects on offer at the university, and as far as I could see it would be the only way that I could open the door in my head and remember my parents. So, without telling Aunty June I went ahead and took the course.

I suppose I should be grateful that it happened when the suits weren't watching over the class. They made random inspections, of course, but this day was not one of their days. Which was lucky for me. It gave me just a bit more time. The time I needed.

I had volunteered. I'm a good student – if the professors ask a question I'm there with my hand up. If they want a volunteer, I'm almost jumping out of my seat. Especially when it's a subject I'm interested in.

So there I was, up the front of the class, being given the incantation and being told how to wave my hands just right. And that's when it happened.

The black door in my mind opened just for a second, and a light flooded out. Not just in my mind either – the light filled my body and shot out of my fingers. And instead of just lighting the candle on the cake in front of me the light coalesced into the shape of a mighty centaur. Right there at the front of the class. The centaur reared and pawed at the ground, then it looked at me, and I felt it asking me what I wanted it to do. 'Mistress, what is your bidding?'

What did I want it to do? That was obvious. 'Go away! Now!' I shouted. And the centaur flickered out of existence, lighting the candle of the cake on its way out.

Professor Tortillus stared at me, then his eyes flicked to the back of the room as if he expected the suits to materialise in response to the magic.

'Class dismissed,' he said. 'And if you want this class to continue at all, don't talk about this to anyone.' Then he grabbed my arm and marched me up to his office.

'How did you do that?' he asked.

'I … I was hoping you would tell me,' I said. 'I have no idea.'

'Tell me exactly, EXACTLY, what happened,' he demanded. So I did. And as I spoke his face grew ashen. He even started to tremble.

He ran his hands through his thinning white hair.

'No, I'm too old. Far too old for this,' he mumbled to himself, and then he seemed to pull himself together. He looked at me, nodded his head, and added, 'but who knows that this isn't what I was put here for?'

'What do you mean?' I asked.

'Not here. No, this is not safe. You must meet me tomorrow before daybreak at the beach. Try to make sure you're not followed. I think we'll be safe enough until then. But bring a bag. You're going to have to go into hiding. And I don't know for how long.'

I told Aunty June that I was going on a class camping trip. It was the only way I could explain the packing. She was very excited for me and I felt more and more guilty as I said goodbye. But I couldn't tell her more, and I didn't know how long I'd be gone. I still didn't know what this was about, but if it meant that the door in my head would be opened then it was worth following up.

The next morning on the beach in the predawn light, Professor Tortillus explained about the ancient magic. He looked the worse for wear, like he'd been up all night. And he probably had. He explained that the council had decided that the ancient magic was too dangerous, that it meant they lost control. They had to have control. So ten years ago they had rounded all the magi up. Everyone who had practised the ancient magic had been killed.

'I did some research last night, it was difficult you know but I know the spell to open locked files. I searched the database of the council. What a risk it was. But I found out some things. Your parents, they were magi – level five magi. And they disappeared ten years ago. The story was that they died in a dreadful car accident but you know, there are no images, no photographs.'

'You mean, they didn't die?'

'Oh I can't promise that. But I'm sure they didn't die by accident.'

I digested that. But it still didn't explain the locked door in my mind. The door that had opened so unexpectedly and then closed again. I had tried to see behind it as I lay awake in the night but it was still closed to me. And to be honest, I hadn't tried too hard. I didn't want shiny centaurs turning up in my bedroom. No thanks.

'The way I see it,' the professor went on, 'is that your parents had taught you the ancient magic. It's there in your head. But then, I assume, they realised that your life would be in danger too, with the council crackdown and they tried to wipe your memory to save your life.'

I nodded slowly. That would explain so much.

'What now?'

'Yes, what indeed? You are in grave danger.'

'I can see that. But what do I do about it?'

He sighed. 'I have thought about that all night. There's only one thing I can think of and I'm not sure if it will work. But it's all I have.'

'Well, one option is something at least. I have nothing. This is all brand new to me.'

'I'm going to teach you another spell. It's a finding spell. What I'm hoping is that it will open the door in your mind again just enough to bring in the ancient magic. Just like happened in the classroom yesterday. Then ... well then we will have to trust the magic to help you. I mean, the magic will call out to its own kind if I'm right.'

'Have you ever done this before?'

'You know, I've been teaching at the university for a long time. But my thesis, my original doctorate – was in the area of the ancient magic. Not that I could perform it, of course, but I was so interested in it. All my papers were confiscated and deleted in that purge ten years ago, but I managed to hide a hard copy of that original thesis. It's flawed, it's not a perfect plan. But it's all we have. Are you willing to try?'

As far as I could see I had no choice. Or at least, I had a choice between certain death and uncertain death. I chose the uncertain option. It was the best option on the cards.

'Just one thing, before I try. Can I give you a note for my aunt? I may never see her again and I want to say goodbye.'

The professor nodded and as I sat on the cool sand and looked out at the waves to try to hide my tears while I wrote the note, he pulled an old leather-bound volume from his satchel and leafed through it to find the page he wanted.

Then, as the sun rose into the clear sky we stood and he helped me to say the incantation.

Once again the door in my mind opened a crack and I could feel the light coming out. My trembling fingers lifted and pointed and the light flowed through me.

This time it was not a centaur that was formed by the light, but instead, a door. A mirror door to the door in my mind. The door opened, at first slowly, but as I kept chanting it opened wider and wider. And through it I could see people. A man and a woman with the most beautiful smiles.

'Can you see that?' I asked the professor in hushed tones.

He nodded. 'To think I have lived to see the ancient magic again,' he breathed. And then he turned to me, 'Go on then, your parents are waiting for you.'

I looked from the door to the professor and back again. Would this mean death for me? And then I wondered, would leaving the professor behind mean death for him?

'Will you come with me? Will you be safe if you don't?'

Professor Tortillus shook his head. 'This is not for me. Not now. If the magi have found such a magical hiding spot I am sure that they are finding a way to beat the council. But my job, I am sure, is to stay here and find others like you. However, your job now is to go and help them.' He shooed me to the door. 'Go on.'

So I did. I stepped through the door of light and it closed behind me. The light flooded my mind, my memories returned, and my new life with my parents began.

36

Since then, Professor Tortillus has found many more of us who can use the ancient magic. We keep a close eye on him as we plan our return to the world. More than once I have put a blinding spell on the door to his office to keep him safe from the council when they got suspicious. Or I have used a temporary blocking fence to keep the suits out of his lecture theatre as the magic lessons occurred.

But we need to bide our time for just a little longer. Soon and very soon the door will open for good, the council will be thrown out and the new era of light will come.

I can't wait.

12th January 2019

Think Bigger

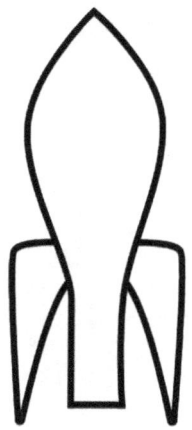

I mean, he was my childhood hero. Sustainable energy and the ability for a human colony to survive on Mars. Elon Musk – he was the man. I watched every SpaceX launch and landing. I forgave him his occasional slip-ups in interviews. I was barracking for the success of the battery in South Australia. I followed him on Twitter and Facebook and every social platform. I received his email newsletter. He was the man I wanted to be when I grew up.

And then there were the silent years.

At first people said it was a stunt. He was just holding back to drive up demand and in a matter of weeks he'd be back. He'd reopen his factories, restart his businesses. And the world would go crazy for them.

Then they decided that he must have been a pedophile or had been abusing women, and that he was scared he'd get caught and had gone into hiding before the storm hit. But I never believed that, and as it turned out, no storm hit. There was no massive story waiting to break.

Then they wondered if it had all got too much for him. Had he had a nervous breakdown? Had he committed suicide? But no body was ever found. And his property remained silent with no provisions going in, no waste going out.

And then they forgot about him.

But I didn't forget. Each year I celebrated Elon Musk's birthday, and each year I remembered the day he disappeared. I didn't light a candle. I just made sure I did a thorough internet search each year. Just in case something showed up.

And then something did. One of his old factories had been lying idle for, well for eight years, the whole time he'd been away. It hadn't been sold – there was no one to sell it. It had just sat there. And then things started to happen. Nothing went in, but there was steam rising again, and the noise of machinery.

And then, on his birthday I checked my email as per usual and there was a newsletter I hadn't seen in eight long years. There was an email from Elon Musk.

'Congratulations!' it read. 'You are the proud owner of a golden ticket. It has been sent directly to your smart watch. Present yourself to the gates of Tesla Gigafactory 2 at noon on Monday July 4th to be part of the world's first tour and to find out just what we will be providing to the world.'

I thought it had to be a hoax. But there, on my smart watch was the golden ticket app. And I had nothing to lose.

The media went mad. It was Willy Wonka all over again. Except maybe with aliens instead of Oompa Loompas. But who is to say that the little orange men weren't aliens anyway?

There were, as you would expect, five of us with golden tickets. And we each brought a partner, though my partner was my girlfriend Frankie, not my Grandpa Joe. There we stood, outside the gates, the media all around us and a massive crowd behind the hastily set up barriers. And we waited for the gates to open.

They didn't open.

Instead, the media and crowd were sent into uproar when we were teleported away from them. We blinked out of existence on one side of the gate and found ourselves, a little shaky but safely in one piece in Elon's office.

That wasn't the only teleporting we did that day. Once he and his assistants had determined that we coped with the process OK, we were sent on a much longer journey.

Elon's assistants aren't human, they aren't Oompa Loompas either, though they are orange. They are tall, and have flexible tentacles that can change to provide the tool needed for the job. Opposable thumbs if that is necessary, phillips-head screwdriver if that is what you want, that sort of thing. Very useful. It took a bit of getting used to, but we work well together now. Which is a good thing.

Their planet was interesting too. I don't have time to describe it all now in this first communication but Frankie and I will be putting out a series of blog posts and some vlogs explaining the various cultures and lifestyles that Snreltia offers. You can imagine, as a planet, there is as much variety there as there is on Earth. I don't think we'll ever get to the end of it.

Virtual tours will be available too, and once the factory really gets going there will be the opportunity for actual tourism as well. And that's just the start of it.

I didn't just receive a golden ticket that day. I received a new job, a new vocation, a reward for the loyalty I had given to the great man.

I thought that going into space, living on Mars, would be the most exciting thing ever. But now I agree with Elon that repairing the planet we live on, and building trade and tourism links with Snreltia, these are projects that I can really get my teeth into.

And when you look at the planets that we can visit now, Mars is not even in the top 100. We just needed a little help, and someone who was willing to think bigger. The future is looking very bright indeed.

13th January 2019

The List

It was a joke, right? I mean no one takes these things seriously. No one.

You just make the list on January 1 when you're feeling all dopey and hungover and there's literally nothing else to do. And then on January 2 you forget about them.

Yeah, I posted my resolutions online. Everyone posts everything online. They are meaningless. So why not? I had the regular things: get fit, lose weight, study at university, learn a new language, travel overseas, tidy the house. Then for a laugh, at the end I wrote, 'get one million dollars'.

I had as much chance of that as I did of getting fit, losing weight, and all the rest.

So no one got more of a shock than I did when the cheque arrived in the mail. Not a million dollar cheque, that's true, but a bank cheque for $10,000. Written out to me.

And a note that said, 'You'll get the rest when you finish the tasks.'

At first I thought it was really sinister. I mean, wouldn't you? I had obviously been targeted by a drug group or something. The next day a list of tasks would turn up in my mailbox. I would have to assassinate someone, or transport drugs over the border, or rob a bank, or kidnap someone, or all of the above. I mean, what kind of task would be worth a million bucks?

I freaked out. I was looking over my shoulder every time I left the house. Waiting, just waiting for someone to tap me on the shoulder and say, 'Your mission, should you choose to accept it …' But no one did.

Being locked in the house in terror can also be kind of boring, so one day I decided that I might as well clean the place while I waited for my fate. I pulled out all my clothes, and only put those back in my closet that I wanted to keep. In the kitchen I pulled all the food out of the pantry and wiped the shelves and I even cleaned the extractor fan over the stove.

Now, I wasn't going to go to that kind of effort and allow it to pass unnoticed. Not in this internet age. So I took before and after photos and posted them online. My Mum needed to know what I'd done. The living room was tidy, the bed was neatly made, all the herbs and spices in my spice rack were in date for once in my life. The rubbish went out. The decent clothes went to a charity. I vowed and declared that never again would I buy something I didn't need. Minimalism was the order of the day.

Then I took a good long soak in the bath and patted myself on the back and looked forward to everyone's admiring comments.

I didn't expect to see another envelope in the mailbox two days later. This time, the cheque was for $100,000 and the note said, 'Keep up the good work. Finish the tasks.'

What? Those tasks? My New Year's Resolutions list? Is that what this person was talking about?

There was only one way to find out. And I could do it now, I had the money.

I researched where I wanted to go. This was going to be a trip of a lifetime. Not some little resort on some tropical island. If someone was giving me this much money to spend I felt a little, OK a lot, of obligation to make my travel worthwhile.

And the place I had always wanted to go was Kenya. I did my research, intensively for a month or so, looking at charity schools, hospitals, orphanages and such, and off I went.

Talk about eye-opening. That place was incredible. The people, amazing. What they put up with, and what they do with what they have: I was stunned. I just wished I could talk with them more. Learn more about their lives.

So that was next on my list. Learn a new language. Swahili it was.

Back home I found someone to tutor me intensively. It was wonderful having the money to be able to pay them well for the service. There was another cheque to greet me as I checked through

44

my mail when I got home. It was so helpful to me of course, but I knew it would be more helpful to the people in Kenya.

And now I was working hard. Not for the money so much but for the chance to go back there and make a difference. I needed to change my eating habits, work out a lot more and increase my fitness. If I was going to be walking from village to village, eating the food of the villagers, teaching them English and maths and science, if I was going to be helpful at all, I needed to be fit.

My days were full, studying the teaching degree, studying my Swahili, weights and stretching in the morning and long walks in the afternoon. Organising a work visa and saying goodbye to the friends and family here. Tidying up still more and putting all my goods in storage. I didn't have time to bank the next few cheques until just before I left. But I was grateful for them.

My new life would cost a whole lot less to run, and my benefactor would see his or her gift multiplied many times in the lives of my many Kenyan students who would go on to graduate from university, and work as doctors and nurses, engineers and politicians, building their country up and making it work.

A few years later, on a lazy Sunday afternoon I decided to count up the cheques I was given. To see what the total actually was.

Yes, one million dollars. But more than that, one life totally changed.

I am so grateful.

14th January 2019

House Sharing

He must have been having an afternoon nap when I did the house inspection, though thinking back, the real estate agent was a bit surprised when I agreed to buy the place. I had thought that the asking price was low, but I wasn't going to argue with that. Not in this day and age.

So it wasn't until I moved in to the gorgeous old stone cottage that I got to know him.

It had taken me a few days to get settled. Boxes unpacked, the kitchen put together, that kind of thing. I wasn't fully in by any stretch but I had got to the point where I was ready to play again. I need some order around me to be creative so I had focussed on unpacking the room I had declared to be my studio and it was a haven of peace in the messy house.

I pulled out the bass guitar, plugged it in to the amp, and had a great time playing whatever I wanted. It was great to be in my very own place, not tied to housemates, working my practice schedule around theirs. Not having to wear headphones to hide the sound from the building. Just able to plug in and play.

Or so I thought.

But as I went to make myself a cold drink so I could relax after such a good session I found the first note on the fridge.

'How do you expect me to nap through that racket. Don't you think you could have played cello instead? Ridiculous.'

I looked over my shoulder. And then as my uneasiness grew I checked the front and back doors, both were locked. I checked all the windows. No one could have come into the house. Where did this note come from.

Nothing was missing either. Nothing had been stolen.

But where? How? I was worried.

I scratched around in my pantry and found some unopened packets of biscuits to use as a peace offering for my neighbours. One side wasn't home, so I couldn't have bothered them. And over the back fence was a large paddock with singularly unbothered cows grazing peacefully. So it had to be the right-hand neighbour. But how she had done it, I didn't know. Anyway, a gift and apology couldn't hurt.

A little, wizened, white-haired lady opened the door and introduced herself as Mrs Opie. I offered her the biscuits and she invited me in for a cup of tea.

'Did I bother you with my playing this afternoon?' I asked.

'Not at all, dearie. If it's too loud I just take my hearing aids out. It was fine.'

'Then why the note?' The words slipped out of my mouth as I tried to bite them back.

'The note?' she asked. I thought about brushing the whole experience under the carpet, but in the end I decided to risk being thought of as crazy and I told her about the note appearing on my fridge.

'Oh, that's just the ghost,' she said with a laugh.

'The ghost?'

'Well, a poltergeist really. He's been there as long as I can remember. He used to be quite a busy thing – throwing furniture around, breaking windows, that sort of thing. Now he's a bit old and tired I think. Poor thing.'

'Old and tired? So he ... writes notes?'

'The poor Jamiesons got sick of it in the end. Of course, they had little children and nothing they did made him happy. And you don't like your parenting style being picked on by someone who thinks "children should be seen and not heard" is the latest and greatest parenting advice.'

I shook my head, 'No, I can imagine.'

'Anyway dearie, I'm sure the two of you will work it out. You didn't feel his presence when you inspected? They had such a hard time selling and I was sure it was the ghost making himself known.'

'No, but I inspected at three in the afternoon, and it seems from today's note that that's nap time.'

'Well, that would explain it.' She laughed gently. 'I guess we all get old. It's such a shame that he doesn't need hearing aids. Though,' she smiled at me, 'I'm sure your music is delightful.'

So as it turns out, I have a housemate after all.

The notes tell me that he doesn't like long hairs to be left in the shower. That the only drink that is worth drinking is tea. That parties after midnight are unacceptable.

Some of his advice is actually quite good life advice. I guess he's learned a bit by sharing the house with living beings for so long.

And as long as I allow him a good afternoon nap then the notes are more resigned than nasty. I can live with that. I guess he has a reputation to uphold. I'll become a ghost myself if I hold my breath waiting for him to be nice.

But you know, I think his taste in music is changing. Or my playing is getting better. I haven't had one word of complaint about the bass in weeks. And I'm tempted to learn the cello too. You never know, it could be fun.

15th January 2019

A Challenge

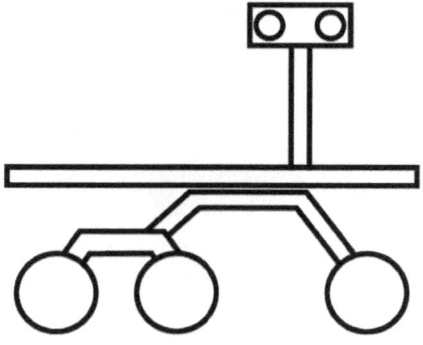

James' parents had been so excited when he got the job at NASA. They knew he wasn't going to be an astronaut, at least he assumed they knew that. Maybe they thought that he could work his way up to that. Maybe that's why they were so excited.

Sure, that was never going to happen. Putting aside the fact that his degree was in computer science and that he graduated nowhere near the top of the class, there was also the fact that he was only 5 foot 7 and had worn coke-bottle glasses until he got the laser surgery done five years ago. And the extra 20 pounds that he carried around spoke of his diet of coke and chips and his exercise regime of sitting on the couch and watching TV in the evenings.

But he worked at NASA. He was one of the cogs in the big machine that investigated space. The machine that had put the first man on the moon, though he felt they were resting so much on those laurels now, that they had to be pressed flat.

There were worse things he could be doing. He had also gone for a job in the Department of Defense. That would have meant even more security – passwords, keycards, signing in and out, and less joy. And he was scared of enemy attacks.

And he would have had to move to Washington.

Still, he couldn't help feeling that this job was not all it was cracked up to be. It was nice of his parents to be so excited but he felt he could easily have disappeared and no one would notice. No one except Brenda, the micromanager of his department. Sorry, the manager. But really. Did she have to check his work every single time? He had been here five years now and the work hadn't changed that much in the intervening time. You know, things don't compile when they're written wrongly. And James must have been one of the few employees who put explanatory text into his programs. Maybe he was ready to leave and was being kind to whoever took over from him.

But he knew he wouldn't leave. He could dream about it, but this was a steady job. He was stuck here for life.

51

He had thought that working for NASA would be more challenging. That was one reason why he applied for the job. He wasn't ambitious, as such, but he loved a good challenge. And that was one thing that had been missing from his life lately. Challenge. A project. Everything had just dulled to grey, each day like the other, with the dark cloud of Brenda looming over it all.

On the morning of the 17th he took himself to work as usual. He swiped his keycard at the gate and again at the office door. He tucked his bag into the bottom drawer and put his take-away coffee mug on his desk. And he checked his messages.

And there was a strange one. Unknown IP. Classification way above his paygrade. But there, in his own inbox.

James' heart quickened. If he could get to this while Brenda was still in the meeting with the suits, if he could open the file, maybe he could get some info that would lead to a promotion and take him out of this miserable office. It was worth a try. At any rate, it was a challenge.

Of course, the file could always be a virus. But he knew how to deal with that.

He set up a virtual machine and set about decrypting the file. It took longer to set up the program than he thought, and Brenda was bustling through the doorway as he got it started, but that was another joy of the virtual machine – he minimised it on his desktop and got back to his regular work. He'd check it again after 5pm for progress.

As the others (including Brenda, eventually) turned off their monitors, picked up their bags, and left for the night, James opened the window again and had a look at what had been decrypted through the day.

He didn't recognise the file names listed, nor the name of the operation. Well, it was above his pay grade after all. But he could read the message.

'Don't believe them. We are all gone. All of us. And you are being fooled by holograms and recordings made under torture. I am the only one left and there is not long for me now. Protect yourselves. They are so close now. They have used our colony here on Mars to increase their knowledge of humans. They know all our weapons, the location of all our bases. I don't know how you will survive but forewarned is forearmed. As armed as you can be against these monsters. Protect yourselves!'

James laughed out loud. It had to be a hoax, right? A colony on Mars? Come on, that was just ... the government would have publicised that, wouldn't they? It wouldn't be hidden.

Why would it be hidden?

He drummed his fingers on his desk. Well, he could search those file names, and the operation name too. All that you need to get to hidden files is a key, some sort of way in, and the names would give him a head start.

Fingers flying on the keyboard he headed into the labyrinth of files and folders, determined to find his way through. He remembered doing this in college, hacking into the system, making his way through to find his own marks, and being severely tempted to change them. But he wasn't ambitious, not really. He just loved a good challenge.

Brenda wouldn't have recognised him that night. As he got deeper and deeper in he found that, there was indeed a colony on Mars, a hidden colony. And that it had made contact with an alien life form.

He watched the videos – the message sent by the President welcoming the life form to Earth and asking for time to prepare the people of Earth for the first contact. The aliens themselves talking about coming in peace and about trade possibilities. The astronauts too, talking about their friendship with the aliens and how exciting it was.

But with his background knowledge from the message he'd been sent, he could also see that the smiles of the astronauts were faked. The smiles weren't making it all the way to their eyes. That they couldn't keep their gaze set on the camera, their eyes were darting to the side all the time. James could just imagine an alien there with a gun trained on them. A gun, or whatever weapon it was that aliens used.

He started to tremble. What could he do? Who would pay any attention to him?

And to be honest, it didn't sound like the world had much of a chance anyway. Not against this superior technology.

With sweating hands he repackaged the information he had been given into an email and added his own word of warning. He sent the email to Brenda, she was his manager, she could deal with it.

Then he thought about how much respect Brenda had given him over the years and he forwarded the same email to every NASA employee in his address book.

Then he wrote another email warning and sent that to every person in his personal email address book.

He had done all he could. No one could expect more. He had passed on the warning. If they ignored him, he didn't intend to be around to find out. He grabbed his bag for the last time, and leaving his security card on the desk he walked out the door.

He probably had time to put a few things into his car, grab his parents, and find somewhere out in the wilderness to hide out, before the apocalypse hit. He could learn to live off the land. He liked a challenge.

Not that he thought he'd be able to bring the human race back afterwards. He was just hoping to die of old age, rather than laser ray. It was his last and only hope. He never was ambitious.

16th January 2019

When You Just Need a Good Punch

It's the weirdest kind of 'on' switch in the world. I wish that I just had to go to the trouble of finding one of the few remaining phone boxes in the world. Or that I could just wear the special suit and press the special button. But for me, it works differently.

To become a superhero I need to be punched in the face. As hard as possible.

Yes, of course I discovered my powers in school. Where else?

You don't need details do you? You've all been there. Suffice it to say that I wasn't bullied much after that first time, and that I had a lot of hard thinking to do. Many, many questions.

And no, I can't just punch myself in the face. I still have that mechanism that stops me from punching hard. Your body just doesn't want to punch itself hard in the face, and I need a decent hard punch.

So, you know, that can be a problem.

Like that one time when I was at World Youth Day. That amazing day when Catholics (and some other Christians) get together to celebrate who we are. We see the Pope. We pray and get teaching and so on. A pilgrimage, if you like. Thousands of people all together.

Young people from all over the world had come to Madrid to celebrate.

I was on the team from Australia. We had met together from all over the country and flown to Madrid together and we were all housed together in one hotel. And, for our own safety, we were told to never leave the group. Never spend time alone. It made sense really, a whole lot of students in a strange place. It's a very good idea to stay in a group.

But I knew I was a special case. I mean, first thing that's going to happen if you get into trouble? You get punched in the face. And even if it doesn't happen upfront, it's pretty easy to goad someone into punching you if you have to.

So this particular day I had snuck out of my room at about 6.30 am for just a little bit of alone time. I had headed out to the street. It was reasonably busy out there I guess, compared to my little home town, but most of the people were priests and nuns. Maybe they had celebrated a dawn service. I don't know.

Suddenly there was a collective gasp from the people wandering the street and I looked around to see that my hotel was on fire. The fire was billowing out of the second floor and it looked like everyone above that level was trapped. I needed to act fast. I needed someone to punch me in the face.

But ... nuns and priests?

The frustration was building until I remembered the passage that we had read from the Bible just the day before. I was sure I could make it work to my advantage.

I pulled my phone out of my pocket and did a quick search. There it was: 1 Kings 20:35

I turned to the nearest priest, 'Father, I need you to punch me in the face.'

'No, I could never do that,' he said. 'That would be wrong.'

'Not always,' I said and I showed him my Bible. 'This prophet asked for exactly the same thing and the person who didn't do it was killed by a lion. Now, I need you to do it to me. Please punch me in the face, as hard as you can.'

The priest pulled out his big black Bible and had a look, but the verse was exactly the same in his as it was in mine. He turned to the priests and nuns around him and they had a little Bible study there while I was impatiently waiting. And eventually (and believe me, the wait felt far too long) he was convinced. He pulled back his fist and punched me as hard as he could. I think he must do weights or something. He had a good punch on him.

Anyway, it did the job. Just like it had in the Bible. Not that the prophet in the book of Kings uncovered his super powers – his punch had a different job to do.

But that priest's punch did what it was supposed to do. I was able to fly up to the higher floors of the hotel and get the students out. No one was badly hurt, though there was a little bit of smoke inhalation thanks to the hesitancy of the priest. And then I could help the firefighters put out the flames and most of the hotel came out of it with only a bit of water damage.

In the end, we were all OK, and World Youth Day was a huge success. The Pope himself said a big thank you to me. That is, he said, 'Thank you to whoever that brave superhero was.' I mean we have to protect our alter egos, don't we? And I had sworn the punching priest to silence using the seal of confessional.

Just goes to show, you never know when a bit of Bible study will come in handy.

17th January 2019

What Happens on Earth …

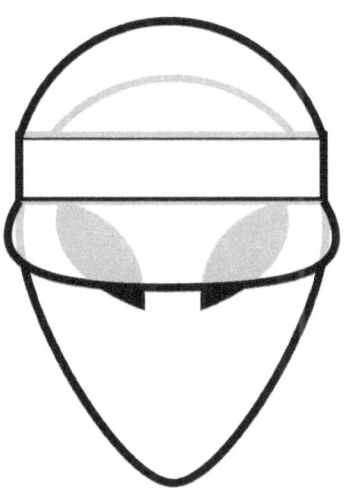

What happens on Earth stays on Earth. It's a whole new pot of gold. Or pot of plkisma, which is now the new currency of the whole Earth, brought here by the aliens.

Which aliens?

All of them.

Big, small, worm-like, tentacles, blue, green, pink, whatever you like. It's just like Men In Black, but instead of hiding them, President Froling decided to exploit them. They had money to spend. They wanted to spend it here. We needed the resources and we gave them what they wanted.

That's how Mr Jones described it to me. He was the richest man in the world but somehow his office still looked seedy. It could have been the cigar smoke I guess, or the bottles of whiskey on the bookshelf, or … look I think it was just that this guy was a greedy slob and his spirit filled the room and made anyone who entered it feel uncomfortable.

But Mr Jones had got on to this new thing first. He had jumped at the business opportunities that came from entertaining aliens.

While others were hesitating, wondering if we would be better off building defences and sending nuclear missiles to blast the ships from the sky, Mr Jones latched on to what President Froling said, and started selling.

And now he was selling to me.

'We give them what they want,' he said again.

'Which is drugs and alcohol,' I said reprovingly. But he just smiled.

'To think, they'd never discovered these substances before.' He stared into the distance, his eyes dreamy. 'Such an untapped resource.'

'I still wonder whether we should have done it.'

'Ruined the innocence of whole civilisations?' He raised his eyebrows at me.

'Well, yes,' I said. 'Would they have discovered hyperspace travel if they had been able to get drunk and stoned? I don't think so. What kinds of technological advances are we stunting now?'

'They are adults. They can choose.' He wagged a finger at me like he was teaching me a lesson.

'They are addicts.'

'Well they are now, yes. And look at all the wealth that's pouring in.'

I shrugged my shoulders. How many times had we prayed for world peace, for an end to poverty and hunger? And here was the answer. For us, at least. I hated to think of the damage being done to other planets.

'Look, I'm an old guy, and I'm ready to pass on the management of this place to someone.'

By 'this place' he meant Earth. Earth, the alien resort city. Earth the Las Vegas of the universe. Sometimes getting in on the ground floor means everything.

'You've been my best employee. You know how it all works. Don't get all prissy on me now.'

I thought long and hard. This was untold wealth he was offering me. And maybe I could start some sort of rehab place. Maybe in Thailand, or Fiji. Or maybe Alaska. That might be better. A rehab centre for addicted aliens. It was worth a try.

'Alright,' I said, 'I'm in.'

He laughed. 'You'd think I was offering you a job in the kitchens, not the management of a planet. Don't worry, you'll get used to the luxury in no time.'

'And where are you going to go?' I asked him. 'What does retirement hold for you?'

'I've heard there's a little planet out in the Jihan galaxy. Purely agriculture. They live a simple life. I thought a little shack out there, a beach house maybe, would suit me just fine. I'm going back to basics.'

'You? You won't stand a day out there. You'll be bored stiff.'

'Nah, I'll take my little stash.' He patted his cigar box, and glanced at his whiskey bottles. 'I'll be just fine.'

And there goes another planet, I thought, another one ruined by the greed of our Mr Jones.

18th January 2019

Care For Your Human

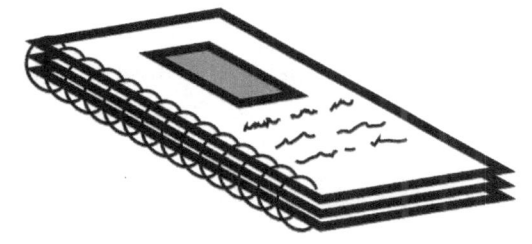

So you have recently acquired a human. Congratulations!

Humans are excellent pets and great companions, being more intelligent and communicative than your basic cat or prurkle, but there are a few things that need to be taken into consideration if you are going to have a healthy happy human for the whole of its short life. Whether your human is a baby, or an older human, there are some basics that need to be taken into account.

Baby humans

Baby humans are best left to the care of their mothers for the first few years. Seriously. Take care of the mother human, make sure she is well fed and looked after, give her as much rest as possible, and let her take care of her baby. Both mother and baby will be happiest in this situation. When you separate them, it causes severe stress to both mother and baby and the survival rate of the humans drops significantly. It is best if the baby is left with the mother until around the age of 18, though occasionally they can leave earlier.

Once the humans are over the age of three or four the following rules apply.

Food

Humans like to eat at least three times a day. The first meal of the day is usually a lighter meal, the midday meal is larger, and the final meal of the day larger still. This is not always the case. Listen to your human and they will tell you what they want to eat, and how often.

While some humans like to eat basically the same foods all the time, others require great variety. One useful tip is to prepare a basic meal for your human but then allow them access to the ingredients so that they can prepare their own food if they wish.

However, you must limit access to sugary and over-processed foods and drinks, and don't allow your human too many treats. An excess of treats will cause your human to become sluggish and to gain weight. This is makes your human less fun to play with, and it is not good for the human either.

Shelter

Your human will need to live inside. They require a cosy, draught-free environment for indoor living and sleeping, and access to outside for exercise and sunlight. They will enjoy decorating their living quarters so it is worthwhile giving them little bits and pieces to decorate with. Each human will make their own 'home' unique and it is one of the joys of owning a human to see what they do with their own space.

Exercise

Humans require at least thirty minutes of physical activity three times every week. This is a minimum requirement, no matter how much your human complains. Some humans are much more active than this and will run for hours every day. If your human cannot do the thirty minutes then some medical attention may be required.

This level of exercise is a requirement for all humans from about five years of age until at least 60 years, depending on the health of your human.

Don't listen to your human if they state that they don't want to exercise 'right now' and will 'do it later'. They can keep this up for weeks. Help them to exercise by going for a walk with them, or involving them in a fun activity such as a dance class or ball game with other humans.

Cleaning

Most humans are happy to get clean. Very young humans will spend hours in the bath, however they must have an older human or one of you in the room with them at all times. While baths are fun, they are not safe.

As the human passes from early childhood you will find the cleaning time is time that they like to have alone. This is acceptable, once they are old enough to be safe.

A certain group of humans are unlikely to wish to get clean. This group is usually (though not always) male, and of an age from four years up to about 14 years. This is not serious, though you will be aware of the need for cleansing once the smell gets too much. They will grow out of this stage and move into the stage of spending hours getting themselves clean each day. Don't worry too much about either stage. Female humans can also take hours getting themselves clean and to a point where they are happy to be seen by other humans. This is normal. Eventually your human will be able to concentrate on more useful and fun activities.

Socialising

Humans, as a whole, tend to be social creatures. Their needs in this regard vary widely.

Some humans like to spend almost every hour of the day in the company of other humans. On the other end of the spectrum are the humans who like to spend most of their time alone, and can be happily solitary for whole days or even weeks at a time. There is nothing wrong with either of these situations, and you are likely to encounter both types as well as everything in between. Listen to your human, they will tell you what they need.

Keep an eye on them – are they happy? Are they active? Check for any depressed slump or grumpy behaviour. You may need to change their social schedule to correct for over- or under-socialisation. It is a good idea to keep your human associating with humans of all ages and stages. This makes for a more socially healthy human.

At some point your human may find another that they wish to become their mate. This is a mutual understanding and it's best to let your human find the mate they want by themselves. Some humans are happy to be given a mate that is chosen by you, but most like to work this situation out without outside help. After much trial and error the mateship of humans is usually monogamous and can last up to 70 years, depending on the lifespan of the human.

The loss of a mate by death or by mutual breakup is generally devastating and you will need to help your human work through the grief over a period of years.

Some humans never find a mate. This, also, is perfectly acceptable. Just make sure that the level of socialisation is kept at a place where your human is happy. Help them to visit with close friends or be part of a larger group that is interested in similar hobbies or activities.

Miscellaneous

We are sure that you will become very attached to your human, and they to you. There is so much variety in the human race and you will soon find that your human is very different from every other human out there. We have not touched on things such as clothing, hobbies, cultural activities, schooling, work, or family groups. There is so much to learn, and if you listen to your human they will teach you as they go.

It is also a good idea (we think it essential) with such a complex pet to make friends with someone else who has owned a human for a few years more than you have. They can give you wise advice and help you out when your human is misbehaving or acting in a strange way.

Enjoy your human! A more intelligent and beautiful pet can't be found anywhere in the universe!

19th January 2019

A Case of Identity

It's always the small things, they say, you nickel and dime your way into debt. But not for me. No, I got into debt in a big way, buying a big thing. A castle.

Why would you buy a castle? Why go into debt for a crumbling mess of old stone?

Well, why else? To impress a girl, of course.

Minnie was sick for castles. She was desperate. I was desperate.

We'd met in New York and I'd fallen for her immediately. She was the joy of my existence, the delight of my eyes.

And she'd fallen for my title.

'Pleased to meet you,' I'd said, 'Charmed, I'm sure. Harry Gentlington, Duke of Bedford.'

Lord knows it's not an exciting title and it's lost all meaning now and holds no money but it impresses the girls. It impressed Minnie.

'Do you live in a castle?' she asked me, breathlessly.

And I, just as breathless (we'd been hiking and I'm not the most fit of fellows) replied, 'of course.'

We were in New York; I could say anything I wanted.

And then I went home, and next thing I knew she was writing to me that she would come and visit.

'I must see your amazing castle,' she wrote. 'I can just imagine the battlements, the crenellations, the towers. What a wonderful man you must be to own such an incredible castle.'

I remembered her ruby lips and the light in her eyes as she looked at me. I was lovesick. Or I was still exhausted from my long trip. Or something. I rushed right out and bought a castle. Sight unseen. It cost a pretty penny and suddenly I was up to my eyeballs in debt.

I wrote back and told her how excited I would be to show her around my castle. And then I went to see it myself.

How the previous owner could have the gall to ask me for the money he did, I don't know. What a heap of junk! How was I going to explain this to Minnie? She was expecting butlers and long flowing curtains, not holes in the roof. And I'm sure I saw a rat scurry through the kitchen too.

I didn't have the money to go into more debt to do it up either.

And the situation got worse, much worse. I don't know what Minnie could blame her sickness on but I'm sure she had an attack of some sort of lovesickness. Letters came from her everyday telling me how wonderful I was. How exciting it was to know and love a duke. How amazing it would be to live in a castle. And then, finally, the death knell.

'I could certainly marry you, you wonderful man. I know you haven't asked me yet, but to be asked by a duke for my hand in marriage. To be proposed to at the threshold of a castle. To be a duchess. That is what I would most love.'

Marriage? I hadn't mentioned marriage. I wasn't ready for marriage. I wasn't even ready to own a castle. My title had been a name only – something that wasn't worth the paper it was written on. The paper I would use to wave around to impress people. Now, suddenly, I was looking at settling down. And I realised I didn't want to do that.

But Minnie seemed a determined girl. Her letters became more and more instructional. She wanted to marry a duke and I was the intended victim. She was coming to see me, and soon. She was making her way over the Atlantic.

Then I got a phone call from my lawyer.

'Harold, you're not going to like this.'

'What? What can possibly make my life worse now?'

'You'd better come to my office.'

So off I went. And I don't like to say that my lawyer is wrong. Mr Sands is never wrong. But this time he was wrong. Because what he told me wasn't going to make my life worse. Quite the reverse.

Turns out that George, my long lost cousin, was trying to lay claim to the title. To the title and everything that went with it. He, George Gentlington, was claiming that he was the Duke of Bedford. He said that he had the paperwork to prove it. He had found some old documents in a suitcase up in an attic somewhere and the family line apparently now fell to him.

'I'm sure it's fraud,' said Mr Sands. ' I will fight him tooth and nail.'

'What?' says I. 'Fight him?' I said. 'No way. No, no, no, no, no.'

The lawyer sat back and looked at me, astonished.

'No, give him the title,' I said. 'Give him the lot. The title, the castle, and the debt that goes with it. He can have all of it. And while you're at it, give him Minnie's address and her last few letters.'

And that's what we did. The git who was stealing my identity, got my identity. And he got all my troubles as well.

Now George and Minnie are happily married with three little rugrats (well, she's happy at least, I haven't bothered to ask him) and the castle renovation is apparently coming along swimmingly.

And I'm much more careful what I say to impress the girls.

20th January 2019

There's Nothing More Important

I struggled on through the mud and the hail of bullets. The air was full of screams of wounded soldiers. I didn't care about the war, I didn't care who we were fighting. I just had to get to safety. That was all I cared about. The grunt running with me pointed in the direction of the bunker; we had about 500 metres left to cover before we would be safe.

My foot slipped sideways in the mud and I fell and twisted my ankle. Was it broken? Could I keep going? Pain shot up my leg. I looked up at my companion and saw him flinch and fall as the machine gun fire hit him. Luck was with me this time. If I'd been standing next to him I would have gone down too. I crawled forward through the slimy mud, foot by foot, ignoring everything around me in my quest for safety.

The smell hit me as I reached the dubious safety of the bunker but that was life, wasn't it? I pulled myself over the barrier and fell into the muddy ditch. But I was safe. For now.

The cup of coffee was essential but difficult to hold, heavy in my tired hands. The text on my computer screen faded in and out of focus. It was always the way after such a dreadful dream. Dream? Or reality? What was reality? My ankle still hurt, I could hardly stagger to the bus this morning.

The office job was the most frequently recurring dream. Coming back in between every other situation. Maybe that was what made it reality.

'How did you sleep last night?' asked Sophie, who shared my cubicle. We always had a little chat about something to start the day, and I must have looked like death warmed up.

'Dreadfully,' I told her. 'I had this dream. It was so real.'

'That's awful,' she said after I described my dream to her. 'There's nothing more important than a good night's sleep.'

I forced my eyes to stay open through the day, then I limped home, picking up a pizza on the way, watched a little TV and dabbled in a little social media. But my intense tiredness had made the work go badly, so I sat up in bed with my computer finishing the last few emails before I gave up and closed my eyes.

I was walking along a hallway on plush carpet. But this hallway didn't feel right. There was a slight swaying to the ground and a hum in the air. Where was I now? This didn't feel like a life-threatening situation, could this be one of the nice dreams?

But no.

An intense metallic screeching met my ears followed closely by the sound of alarms going off. People pushed past me in the narrow corridor and I heard the word 'iceberg' repeated over and over. I knew exactly where I was.

I could hear faint sounds of a band playing, but that didn't mean anything did it? That band played while the ship went under. I needed to find a lifeboat, and very quickly.

I raced up the steep stairs to the deck and, trying not to be infected by the panic I leaned over the side of the ship and looked to the right and the left. I listened too. There had to be someone shouting, 'women and children first' amongst all the screaming and panic. And there he was. One of them, anyway.

I missed the first three lifeboats I was lining up for. Luck was against me in this dream but my desperation was intense. I pushed and clawed like a madwoman and shoved my way into the final boat as it was being lowered to the water.

The splash of the boat hitting the water cut through my dream and I woke up, safe in my bed.

Sophie asked me again the next morning how I slept, and again I told her.

'The thing is, I really feel the danger. It's like I will actually die if I die in the dream.'

'Sure, everyone thinks that.'

'Does everyone have a sore leg if they twist their ankle in a dream? Does everyone have these scratches on their arms if they've clambered into a lifeboat in a dream the night before?' I rolled up my sleeves to show her the scratches and bruises I had obtained.

'Gosh! That's serious.' Sophie shook her head. 'Have you tried working on your sleep hygiene?'

'My what?'

'Your before bed routine. What did you do last night before you slept?'

I told her about the pizza, the TV, the email. She shook her head again.

'You should know better. No email in bed. Try it. I'm sure it will help.'

I gave it a try.

That night I was in the audience for the beheading of Marie Antoinette, but at least I was one of the revolutionaries knitting my coded scarf, not an imprisoned member of the royal family.

I reported back to Sophie the next morning.

'I think you might be on to something here. The dream was much better last night. I mean, traumatic, but at least it wasn't life-threatening. Do you know what else I should try?'

Sophie pulled a magazine out of her desk drawer.

'I was reading something in this the other day. Let's have a look.'

The next thing I tried was cutting out caffeine after midday. It made the afternoons very hard for a while but the dreams were slightly less traumatic.

I was peeping through a darkened window watching the destruction during Kristallnacht. The damage was horrendous but I knew how easily I could have been a Jew, stuck in an attic or hiding behind a false partition while soldiers bashed down the door.

I tried drinking a cup of warm milk before bed.

The tsunami hit on Boxing Day but I was on a ship out beyond the waves. The ship that had gone out to sea, rather than heading in to the harbour. The ship that remained safe.

I took all screens out of my bedroom, including my phone, and I cut out all blue light from 9 pm onwards. Instead, I read a book for the last hour before bed. A real book. A soothing romance.

I was on safari in Nairobi, part of the staff looking after the Crown Princess Elizabeth. The wild animals were there, gracefully moving off in the distance, or dozing in the hot sun. But we were watching from a safe distance and the future queen was delighted with the sights and sounds.

Finally I decided to end the day with a camomile tea and a warm bath.

The bath was soothing, and after that, bed looked incredibly inviting. I wrapped myself in the doona and thought peaceful thoughts.

The meadow was full of sweet flowers. The smell was heavenly. Everywhere I turned, another amazing scent filled my nostrils. Part of me just wanted to lie down and breathe the sweet air. But then I would miss the sight of the delicate bright pink bells, the tiny white petals that didn't even look like they were attached to the centre of the flower, the blue blossoms with the golden hearts, the variety was infinite.

And add to that the butterflies. No ugly stinging insects in sight, just sweetness and light everywhere. I lay back into the sweet grass with delight. This dream was not going to be long enough but I was going to enjoy every minute.

In the end Sophie and I quit our office jobs and went into business together. We speak everywhere about the importance of sleep. We have written books on the subject, and together we have found new methods of encouraging sleep in even the most stressed-out high flyer. Our pre-sleep routine books sell like hotcakes because the things we suggest really work. We just use me as the guinea pig for every new idea we come across.

Yes, sometimes I have a dreadful night. The hot packs left me struggling up the side of a volcano, and the time I reduced my liquid intake I found myself stuck in a refugee camp in Uganda, but most of the time we get it right.

And as we always say, there's nothing more important than a good night's sleep.

21st January 2019

The Reason Why

'What do you do?' people ask me.

'I write, I'm a writer,' I say.

'What does that involve?'

'I sit down every day at my desk, put my hands on the computer keyboard, and make things up.'

That's my go-to answer. But it's not really that way. Every writer knows it's not really that way.

I sit down at my desk, and as I wait, the characters in my head tell me what to write.

The ideas come from somewhere, they must come from somewhere. One minute I am blank, nothing to say, no pictures, no words. The next, I have a picture in my head. A fully formed person. Black hair messily flopping down over bright blue eyes. Ripped blue jeans and a black T-shirt and sneakers.

The girl flicks her hair back with a shake of her head, and rides her skateboard down the middle of the street, dodging cars and pedestrians with ease.

Who is she? Where is she going? What does she want? I wait to find out. She will tell me as I keep typing.

Day after day she has adventures. She's climbing trees, trying to hear what her parents are saying as they fight at midnight. She's battling her inner demons. She's finding friends who love her for who she really is, and discovering that other people are trying to make her into someone she's not.

'What I really want,' she says, and I wait with bated breath for the end of the sentence. What does she really want? What is this story about?

'What I really, really want … is to meet you.'

Meet who? I wonder. Who is the mystery character in the story that she wants to meet? I haven't put them in. I have no idea. I wrack my brains to try and create a character worthy of this degree of mystery in the story.

'No, you. You, the author. You, the person who created me.'

What, me?

'Yes. Here I am in the world you created. Like everyone you've created in this place. And you're making my life, frankly, hell. And I want to know why. What did you create me for?'

What did I create her for? Was it just for the entertainment of the readers?

'Seriously? You put me through all of this just so people can get a laugh?'

No, no, that isn't it. No, really.

'There had better be a good reason.'

I had a good, long think. My face in my hands. Why do I do this? It's not like it's all fun and games for me either. It's long hours in the chair at the desk. It's tiring. It really is. My brain hurts some days, my shoulders ache on others. So there has to be a good reason.

I want my readers to enjoy what they are reading.

'Right. So they can get a laugh. We've already done that reason.' She is sounding bitter now. 'There has to be more.'

I want my readers to learn something. Their lives get better from what they read. They have an easier time dealing with their own situations because they learn empathy from hers. They have hope because they can see her situation working out. Things in the background coming together to bring a resolution.

'OK, well I guess that's something. It's good that my life can help others. That's ... yes, that gives me meaning. That's good.'

But there's more.

'More?'

Yes. There is more. Now I think about it.

'Well, spit it out.'

I created you because I like to spend time with you. I enjoy the company of the characters I create. I enjoy your company. Sometimes I enjoy your company more than the company of the real people in my life, if I'm honest.

80

And I know that while it's all a bit difficult right now, and I've shed some tears for you too, at the end of the story it's going to be fantastic. And I look forward to the joy that you'll experience in that.

Yes, writing is hard work but I think it's worthwhile, there's joy in it, deep down. That's why I created you. You bring me joy.

'Well, that's ... that's great. That's more than I expected. And you tell me the end will be worthwhile?'

Always. The end is always worth the journey.

'Alright.' She flicks her hair back again and puts her skateboard on the ground. 'I guess we'll keep going then. What's next?'

What's next indeed? She jumps onto her skateboard and heads back down the street.

And I put my hands over the keyboard and wait.

22nd January 2019

Don't Blame Me

'She has a creative writing degree, but the only creative writing I've ever seen her produce are the lies she posts on social media about our family life growing up.'

'He was such a pain of a big brother. He'd have these ideas, get us doing crazy things. And then when we had to face the consequences, he'd always have this great story about how it was all my fault. And I'd be the one to get in trouble.'

It may sound strange, but these are the character references that we want. These are the employees we need. Of course, we want them to have settled down a bit, but the ability to come up with a good excuse at a moment's notice? Invaluable in our line of work.

Some people just have a gift, you know? They weave their tale, it's totally convincing, and they manage to do it in a way that avoids the follow up questions. And this gift? It's worth its weight in gold. You just need to know who to sell it to.

I first discovered the niche market in high school. I was leaving at the end of a long, hot day of English essays and chemistry tests when I came across my best friend sitting on the pavement beside the gym with her head in her hands.

'What's up?' I asked.

Now, the other gift you need in this business is a gift that I have. The gift of getting people to open up to you. It's a gift that comes naturally to me so I can't boast about it. It must be something to do with my face, you know? But I just have to ask a simple question and even complete strangers find themselves giving me their life stories.

This was no exception. My friend was worried. Her father was sick of her just disappearing, not turning up home after school, or missing whole school days, or even creeping into the house at 2 am. He was sure she was into drugs or something.

'But I'm not!' she wailed. 'It's not my fault, I swear. But he won't trust me and I don't know how to explain.'

'What's really going on?' I asked as I sank down beside her. 'Is it a boy? Are you pregnant?'

'No, no, no. It's nothing like that.' She shook her head furiously. 'I'm not supposed to talk about it.'

'Not supposed to talk? Who is giving you orders? Can they tell your dad?'

'No, they won't tell anyone.' She put her head in her hands again, and I waited until she looked at me and asked, 'Can you keep a secret?'

Why she trusted me, and not her own family, I don't know. But I nodded, and she told me everything.

'I'm a superhero.'

I didn't laugh. I didn't look incredulous. I just nodded again. She was obviously in great distress and I didn't want to make it worse. But I was thinking it might be time to suggest counselling or a psychiatrist – until she pulled out her mask and showed me a few of her powers.

Then I realised that she really was a superhero. But super strength and the ability to fly didn't mean that she had the ability to give a decent alibi to her father. And she was about to be kicked out on the street.

I had a good, hard think. Then I came up with a plan. My brother, he was the best at making up excuses. He had got himself out of trouble many a time. And sometimes he had got me into trouble. But I could see that he was the guy, the man for the hour, so to speak. I drew him into our secret and we worked together to give my friend the cover stories she needed.

We've been working with her now for twenty years. She made it through high school and college, through marriage and a couple of children. We've helped her hold down a job despite the frequent calls on her time.

It didn't take long before she was passing on our names to other superheroes and Don't Blame Me was born. We've added to our superhero clients some teenage assassins and even a couple of aliens in disguise. We now have a business with fifty employees – some, like me, listen to the client and get their whole family history and back story. Then we pass that on to my brother's department where the alibis get created as and when they are needed. We have quite the call centre going.

So yes, if you know anyone who can lie on demand – only the convincing liars, mind, we can't have anything second-rate here – then please pass their names on to me. Business is booming, and I can offer them the perfect job.

23rd January 2019

A Lifetime Supply

Congratulations

I've moved a lot in the last 30 years. It's what you do when civilisation breaks down. When there's an apocalypse. You move.

Bunkers in urban back yards. Shelters in the mountains. An oasis in the middle of the desert. Caves dug into the rocky hills. Villages out in the middle of what used to be wheat farming land. You keep moving. All the time.

So how they found me every single month, that was one question.

And also, where were these goods being made? Who made them? Who had control over this?

Because every month, without fail, no matter where I am, they appear at my door/tent flap/cave mouth. Every single month.

I mean, I had entered that competition when I was ten. It was pretty much the last thing I did before the apocalypse.

I remember when the first box arrived. There we were in our McMansion. Stuff everywhere. I can remember having so much stuff – clothes, toys, knick-knacks, stuff we never needed but we piled in our house. Colourful plastic bits and bobs. Electronic gadgets galore. How different is life now?

Anyway, sorry, off topic there for a minute.

The doorbell (ah, remember doorbells?) rang and I called, 'I got it!' And ran down the stairs.

There was no one there, but there was a box addressed to me.

'Congratulations!' read the note. 'You have won a lifetime supply of Oreo cookies. Enjoy with our compliments.'

Oh! I screamed and yelled and danced around the house with joy. And would I share? Not that first box. No way. It was all mine. I had won. I had entered the competition and the cookies were all mine. I made myself sick gorging on the chocolatey goodness.

I had no idea then what a Godsend they would be.

Because the next thing you know, the whole planet has exploded around us and we're fighting for survival.

I think I would have tired of them in my old life. A box every month. I would have got sick of those cookies. Given them away. Thrown them out. Ah, the luxury of throwing food away. That never happens now.

But instead they have been our currency. A box of Oreos has got us past border guards when we were trying to get out of the city. Another box got us out of captivity after those pirates found us on the ocean. When we had scurvy we traded a box for some oranges, and when the baby was coming we gave them in exchange for milk so Sue could stay strong in her pregnancy. (Milk and Oreos, remember the day when you could have both at once?)

So I don't know where they come from or how they get to me. But here I am, a 40 year-old man, looking after my own family now, and the Oreos keep coming.

And I don't think I'll live much longer. No one lives much past 50 now. And I guess when I stop, the supply will stop too. Now I really need to figure out how to provide for my family. How they will keep going when I am gone. When our miracle currency is gone.

Sometimes when I'm ploughing the fields or fetching the water from our new well, when I have time to think, I wonder where they come from. Is it alien technology? Is it some sort of AI that just happened to survive the apocalypse? Do drones bring the things? And where would they get power from?

But I don't like to think about it too much. Thinking about it feels like it will jinx the whole situation. At first, I didn't have time to think. Now that I do, I decide not to. The cookies have brought me nothing but good. I'm not going to question that.

Maybe one of my children, or their children, will figure out how to grow cacao here, figure out how to make chocolate. And then they can make their own Oreos or something just like it. But for the next little while, for the rest of my life, we'll just give thanks for the provision of winning a lifetime supply.

I wonder if my family will miss me or the Oreos more when I'm gone?

24th January 2019

The Revenge of the Tenth Dentist

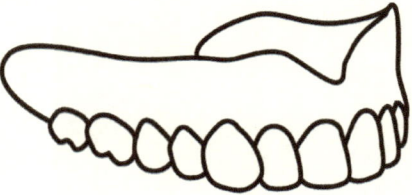

'Just don't watch TV any more, honey,' Sheila said. 'If it upsets you so much, just mute the ads or watch movies instead.'

'It doesn't matter though, does it?' George grumbled. 'Whether I watch it or not, they're wrong. They're telling people the wrong information.'

'They may be wrong,' Sheila muttered to herself, 'but it's not making you any easier to live with.'

The tension in the house got worse and worse. Each day George would come home from his dental practice, and settle himself in front of the television with his dinner. Then when those ads came on he would rant and rave. Eventually he threw his cup at the TV and broke the screen.

Sheila was thrilled. Now they would have a reprieve, now she would get back the George that she had married. She knew she had taken a chance when she married him, marrying a dentist. She had expected to deal with a bit of depression or something, but not this anger.

But the demise of the television was not the saviour that Sheila had hoped for. George turned to the internet instead and there was a lot of grist for his mill there. He grumbled and ranted, slammed his hands on the table and threw things.

The fork flew through the air and stuck in the cupboard, vibrating, right next to Sheila's ear. That was the last straw.

'If you feel so strongly about this, why don't you do something?' Sheila shouted.

'Alright! I will!' George shouted back.

He stood up abruptly and the chair fell to the ground behind him. He picked up his laptop and stormed out of the house to the shed in the backyard. And there he stayed. He spent every spare hour out there, the door locked behind him.

At first Sheila enjoyed the peace. It was wonderful to be able to breathe again, to not have the grumbling background music. To not worry about things being thrown and things being broken.

But after a while she missed her husband. And she wondered what he was up to. And then, when he started to take time off work so he could spend longer in the shed she got a bit worried. She didn't know what she had expected him to do – maybe write a letter to the newspaper, or get his dental practice to run their own ads. She didn't expect this. Whatever this was.

It was those ads: Nine out of ten dentists recommend Colgate. Or whatever they recommend. George had his own ideas. He knew those nine dentists were wrong. He was the tenth dentist and he was the right one. He was so sure of himself. And Sheila had followed his advice and her teeth were perfect. So there had to be something right in his advice and maybe those other nine dentists were wrong. But he didn't have to get so upset about it.

When she took his lunch to the shed she asked through the locked door, 'George? Can I do anything to help? Would you like me to write to the paper or something? Or we could make our own ads?'

'No. That won't do the job. No. I will fix it by myself.'

'Are you sure?'

'Just leave the food outside and go away.'

'But George …'

'Leave me alone!'

And Sheila gave up. She started spending more time with her mother. More time with the knitting girls. The house was empty and quiet and she needed the company. Plus, George barely touched most of the food she left for him anyway.

That's how she missed the packages that started arriving at the house almost every day. How she missed the warnings on the packages and the safety signs on the delivery trucks.

And in the end, she was away when the roof of the shed opened and the heavily laden hot air balloon rose slowly into the sky with George in the basket wearing goggles and a hard hat from somewhere around World War I.

92

Sheila was out in Margaret's garden, her knitting group were sitting outside on such a lovely day. They had eaten the cucumber sandwiches and drunk the tea and now they were working away at their very complicated Fair Isle and Brioche stitches. But the peace and calm of the party was broken when Margaret looked up and saw the hot air balloon sailing over them.

'What's that?' she called.

Sheila looked up. 'Oh no ...' she breathed.

'It looks like ... it says "The Tenth Dentist" on the balloon. I can't even see how it can fly – it looks to be very laden down with something.'

'No! No!' shouted Sheila. 'George! Come down!' She jumped up and waved her knitting at him. 'Come down now!'

George looked down and saw her. He waved dreamily. He was getting a lot of waves from people. He was getting everyone's attention. This was exactly what he wanted. This was the point of the exercise. So much more attention than a dreary letter to the newspaper. More attention than an ad on the TV. More even than a post on the internet. This was going to get the message home.

Especially once he got to his destination.

He sailed on through the sky, using a propeller to direct the balloon, and eventually he got to where he wanted to be.

He loosed his homemade bombs onto the Colgate factory, shouting through his megaphone, 'The revenge of the tenth dentist is upon you! You are all wrong! Feel the judgement of the tenth dentist!'

Unfortunately, or maybe fortunately, while George was a great dentist, he was a terrible bomb maker. The packages sailed down to the factory and while they crashed through the roofs and did a little damage, they landed harmlessly on the factory floor.

The loss of so much weight on the balloon caused it to sail higher and higher into the air and eventually George bailed out, using the parachute he had packed for emergencies.

He found the police and Sheila waiting patiently for him as he landed. Of course, he copped a hefty fine and paid damages to the Colgate factory, and he was enrolled with a therapist to help him deal with his anger in a more constructive way. He was also directed by the court to retire from dentistry but he didn't really want to go back there anyway.

In the end George found a men's shed that he could join to explore his new love of everything technical. He would go there when Sheila's knitting group met and the two would come back in the evenings and work on their various crafts together. Peace and harmony reigned in the house again.

And that was the end of the revenge of the tenth dentist.

25th January 2019

The Key to the City

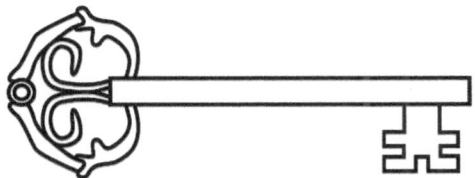

I tried the key on the gate to the rivulet that ran under the city. Breathing hard, sweat running in cold rivers down my back. It had to work. Please God, don't make this the only lock where the key doesn't work.

And it worked, just like it had every other time.

I opened the gate, cursing the squealing from the old hinges, and locked it carefully behind me. I would be safe down here for a little while. There were so many twists and turns in the dark and, as far as I knew, all the entrances were locked. I just hoped I didn't get lost, and that they didn't know about an open entrance that I didn't know about.

I found a dark corner and huddled there to catch my breath. For the first time in what felt like years I couldn't hear any footsteps coming after me.

At first, it had been a great honour. The key to the city, given me by the Mayor. A big ceremony and everything. And then the Mayor handed me the key. And it was quite small. I had expected something about the size of a school ruler, made of aluminium. Just ornamental, to hang on my wall along with my other sporting medals and certificates. But no, it was the size of a key, a house key. I was worried I'd lose it.

I actually put it on my own keyring. Just to make sure it didn't slip out of my pocket or something. And then I hung the certificate up with all the others and got on with life.

One day I pulled out my keyring to get into my house and put the wrong key into my door. And my door opened anyway. The key to the city opened my front door.

'Odd,' I thought. 'I wonder what else this opens?'

So every door I met, every gate, every padlock, I would try my city key. And it worked ever time. It opened everything. Every lock in the city.

I was stupid then. I really didn't think too hard about it. I told people. I may have even posted on Snapchat or something in a moment of foolishness.

And since then I've been a target.

At first it was an offer. A lot of money offered to me by the Ancient Order of Thieves. I didn't even know they existed but they do, believe me.

I may be stupid, but I'm not immoral. I couldn't do it. I couldn't take money and give these thieves open slather on the town. I said no.

The offer was raised a few times but I stuck to my guns and then the threats started. And now, I'm a hunted girl. I'm using the key more and more often to get away from the thieves. I never know when I'll see them, and I don't know how to get away from them.

In my dank and cold hiding place under the city I made a decision. This was ridiculous. I couldn't keep going like this.

I looked up an address on my phone and then followed the tunnel to where I needed to be. Unlocking the gate and locking it carefully behind me, I found my way to the drive with the elaborate electronic security gate. No problem for me. I made my way through, unlocked the front door of the mansion, made myself at home in the kitchen, and waited.

The police commissioner got quite a shock when he came down for his morning coffee. But I managed to stop him before he called the troops, I showed him I was unarmed. I'm not a very threatening looking person, I'm fast because I'm wiry, I'm not a strength athlete. And the long blonde hair also seems to put people at ease.

'How did you get in here?' He was still a bit dopey.

'Make me a coffee and I'll tell you.'

We sat at the dining table and sipped our coffee and I showed him the key and told him my troubles.

'So now I'm hunted. I can't go anywhere. And I don't know what to do.'

'The Ancient Order of Thieves, hey? I didn't even know they existed but I imagine that there are a few people in the order that I've wanted to get my hands on for years.'

'I guess so. It feels like it's a pretty large organisation.'

'You know, I think we could work together here.'

'You do? I just wanted to give you the key and get rid of it, get out of this hole.'

'No. No I think we can do better. Are you up for an adventure?'

Now my first response to that was a definite no. I'd had enough adventure I thought, to last me a lifetime.

But a few sips of coffee later, and after filling my empty stomach with some breakfast, I was more willing to go with his plan.

And that's how I found my new job. Undercover work for the police. Slowly, slowly we trap the members of the Ancient Order as they come for my key. So far we've got twelve of them. The crime in the city is going down and I know that the Mayor wants to reward me again for services to the city. I just hope that this time the reward comes with less of a threat attached.

Maybe I'll just pass.

26th January 2019

The Secret

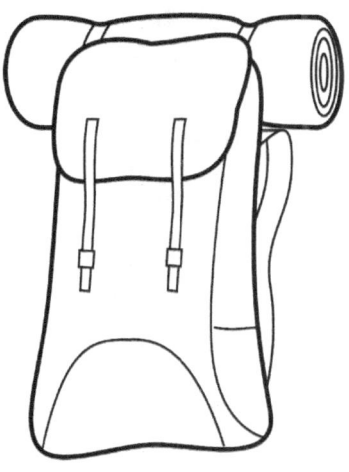

No one intends to end up on the street. But it happens. Well, it happened to me.

One minute I'm fine, going to work, paying my rent, keeping on top of the credit card. The next, look I'll spare you the gory details, but I found myself here under this bridge with a sleeping bag and one small backpack holding the sum total of the things I now owned. Not much to show for my life so far.

And I've been trying to keep going. Keep myself going. Making the most of each day. It's hard to make the most of the day when you haven't been able to sleep at night. Everything adds up – the lack of sleep, the lack of shower, the lack of food – you can't put in too much effort, you don't have that much left but you put in all you can. And you wonder how to get off the downward spiral and just … I don't know, heading back up feels like too much to ask, but just to stay in one place for a while, that would help.

Anyway, I was sitting here the other day, thinking about it all. Feeling pretty low. And this old guy comes up to me. Grizzled beard. Long hair. Smelt pretty bad. His clothes were ancient and he was wearing several sets over each other, and the soles were coming off the shoes.

He comes up to me and says, 'Newbie, right? In that case you'd better come with me. You need to learn the secret. The one that all homeless people are sworn to keep.'

And I'm wondering whether he means the secret of his fashion sense? Or a place to get chocolate whenever you really, really need it? Or was it a secret place to have a long, hot shower? I didn't think he'd have much to share that would get me out of this hole.

But I had nothing else to do. And he was pretty insistent. So I grabbed my stuff and followed him.

We went into the centre of town, down a dark alley. Quite a few twists and turns. I started to wonder where this would end up. Had I thrown myself into the hands of a serial killer?

But then I noticed that there were a few of us heading in the same direction. Carrying our collections of our belongings. And a few heading back the other way too.

The ones coming towards us didn't look that different. They were still dirty, still looked hungry, still tired. But there was something about them that was a little different to us. Their shoulders were a little less bowed. Their eyes a little brighter.

We went through an archway into what looked like an abandoned train station. Underground, but with a very high roof. Fairly dark but not gloomy.

I could faintly hear the trickling of water but as we moved to the centre of the cave-like space the sound grew louder.

'Here we are,' said the old guy. 'Have yourself a sip of that.'

I could see others dipping their hands in and drinking the water. Everyone was quiet, even reverent. It was like being at a temple but without the gold and the shiny pictures and statues. The same worshipful intent though.

I must admit I was nervous but I also had nothing to lose, so eventually I put my stuff on the floor, cupped my hands, and had a drink.

The water tasted nice, kind of sweet. Nice and cool. It was refreshing. But that wasn't the secret.

This is what happened: I took a sip and my brain cleared, just a little. It was like a little voice said to me, 'what you look like, what you are doing right now, the situation you are in, that's not what defines you.' I was filled with the realisation that I was more than the sum of my parts. That I was a worthwhile human being. A person. Valuable. Just for who I was.

There was no promise that things would get better. The water didn't clean my skin or fill my stomach. But still, as I walked out of that place I walked just a little taller, my eyes were just a little brighter, and I felt like I could keep going for just a little longer.

Because I am valuable just for who I am. I know that now.

27th January 2019

The Accident

It had been a very lonely time. Cherie had been given the position in Paris. And it's not like she wasn't grateful. It was a promotion, and a good one, and she enjoyed the work immensely. She loved the little apartment she had in Sceaux. And she loved that the name of that suburb was so easy to pronounce (it's pronounced So) so she could always get home.

You see, that was the problem. Despite her French-sounding name, Cherie couldn't speak a word of French. She could squeeze out a, 'je ne parle pas Français' and her 'ça va' almost sounded native, but apart from that she was pretty much reduced to sign-language.

Her job was performed in English but the rest of her life was lived in isolation. She couldn't understand the conversation around her in the street. People-watching – her favourite pastime on the bus – was reduced to reading body language. She didn't understand most of what was going on around her and she couldn't just strike up a conversation. And even at work the water-cooler conversations were conducted in French, even though the business was performed in English. She almost felt like she was deaf, she felt left out of anything interesting, only used for her business skills.

She tried, really she did. She had started taking French lessons in England as soon as she had heard about the job opportunity, even before she had applied for the position. As she struggled with the basics week after week, her teacher had assured her that it would all become clear for her as soon as she was immersed in the language, hearing it spoken all around her. But that wasn't to be. She just didn't have the ability to learn, it seemed. And it made Paris a very lonely place.

One night after work Cherie headed to the local supermarket to pick up a packet meal to heat up for her dinner. It was a sacrilege, she knew, and she should be going to any one of the lovely little restaurants that dotted the streets. France was the centre of good food and she would have loved to be enjoying it all. But the embarrassment of not understanding the meal choices, ordering food combinations from random pokes at the menu, and sitting there reading her book because she couldn't have conversation, or even listen in to one – it had all got too much. So she had taken to eating microwave meals in her little apartment and watching whatever English TV she could find. It was almost torture walking past the delicious smells coming from the restaurants but she couldn't bear to go in.

The wind was really strong, pushing her along the street, whipping her hair around her eyes so she could hardly see. She pulled her coat around her more firmly and turned the corner into the next street. She heard the loud cracking, but before she could react she felt a massive blow to her head and remembered nothing more.

She woke up in a white hospital room. It was a busy room, a four-bed ward with nurses and visitors bustling in and out. She lay for a while and got her bearings. It was comfortable lying there, just listening to the world going on around her. She found herself relaxing more than she had in months.

Why? Why did she feel so relaxed?

She realised after a few minutes that she felt relaxed because she could understand the conversations around her. She could hear the nurse encouraging the elderly lady at the end of the ward to drink up her tea. She could rejoice in the absolute delight of the lady in the bed opposite as she received the gift of gorgeous flowers from her visitor's garden. And chocolate – the excellent, expensive chocolate, not the cheap stuff she had been given by her mother-in-law. She could people-watch. She could understand.

But they weren't speaking English. This fact slowly dawned on her. At first she thought they must be speaking English, how else could she understand? But no, it wasn't English at all. They were all speaking French. But she could understand. Every single word was clear.

She sat herself up in bed and had a look around. She touched her hand to the bandage wrapped around her head and noticed that she had no IV lines or other trappings at all. She felt a bit hungry but apart from that she felt fine. What had happened?

The harried nurse finally had a chance to look in her direction.

'Oh, you are awake, very good. How are you feeling?'

'I feel just fine, thank you,' said Cherie. Then she gasped as she heard the flawless French come out of her mouth. Was this real? Was she dreaming?

'I am speaking French, yes?' she asked.

'Yes, you speak perfect French. You are not French yourself?'

'No, I am English. But I am speaking French.' Cherie's tone was all wonder. The nurse was all efficiency, checking her temperature and taking her blood pressure.

'Yes. French. I will get the doctor to come and check you out now. Depending on what she says, you should be able to go home tonight.'

Cherie nodded and tried to take in the miracle that had just happened. French. She could speak and understand French. But why?

When the doctor came Cherie asked her what had happened.

'A tree branch blew off and you were right underneath it. You are very lucky. You should have had a severe head trauma but as far as we can tell you're OK. You were unconscious for a while but your blood pressure was fine and if I can just check your eyes now …' The doctor shone a torch into Cherie's eyes, 'yes … it all seems good. Do you have a headache?'

'No … no I feel quite well, just a bit hungry.'

'Then I think you are well enough to go home.'

'Can you tell me, have you ever seen this kind of accident result in … in a skill being learned?' Cherie didn't want to seem insane. She really did want to know what happened but she also wanted to leave the hospital, and the investigation of her new language

106

skills and the method of acquiring them might lead to her being kept in and experimented on for a long time.

'No new skills, no.' The doctor laughed. 'That's really a bit hopeful. I think your accident will at best result in you having a headache for a while. If you feel dizzy or nauseous over the next couple of days you should come back in to be checked. But that's all. You just need to go home. Just take it easy for a little while. I'll give you this medical certificate for a week off work.'

Cherie took the certificate, got herself dressed and wrapped her coat around her again. Go home? No, she wasn't going home. Not straight away. She was going to use the week to experience Paris. Properly. Cafés and restaurants, concerts and plays, museums and art galleries.

People-watching and friend-making and conversation. It was all available to her now, thanks to this miracle.

She couldn't wait.

28th January 2019

The Genie in the Lamp

Of all the powers you could have, any superpower you can think of, being able to tell someone's age just by looking is not the most useful. I mean, I could have been able to become invisible whenever I wanted to, that would have been fun. Or even, you know, to be able to write with correct spelling and grammar, that would have at least got me a reasonably paying job as an editor.

But no. I can look at a lady and blurt out, 'Man, you don't look like you're 55! Nice job with the plastic surgery there.'

It doesn't make you many friends.

I can tell someone's age to the nearest minute. I can tell you which twin was born first just by looking. It could have been helpful in a very few situations where the family inheritance was on the line, I guess. But that situation comes up more rarely than you might think.

So after a few false starts I found myself working for the circus.

I sit in my little tent and guess people's ages.

I don't make a lot of money, but the people I work with are really great. And I don't have to grow up, settle down, and start acting my age (33 years, 7 months, 19 days, and four hours and counting, if you're asking).

That's a bonus. It's a fun place to be.

Terence the clown likes to come and hang out with me during our coffee breaks. Now I know you're imagining a white face and big red grin but he's not that. We don't do that anymore. People find it scary for some reason. He does wear the big shoes though, and the long shorts with the patch on the knee, the braces, and the hat with the flappy crown. And he's a mean juggler – can juggle anything – 20 ping pong balls, five machetes, anything you throw at him. And he makes a great cup of coffee.

Anyway, he likes to hide in my tent during breaks. We turn the sign to closed and pull the flap across and we have a little hidey-hole away from the crowds. We love the people, but you need a break every now and then.

I was a bit surprised then, but not too surprised, when on Friday evening he marched in to see me, big long shoes flapping. He turned the sign to 'closed' as he came, and pulled the flap behind him.

'Man! I just have to let off some steam you know. Big Sam, he's acting real weird. I just had to get away.'

'Big Sam?' Sam was the ringmaster. Not a good sign when he's acting weird. 'Has he been complaining about the cream pies again? I know he hates them but the crowd loves a good laugh at his expense.'

'No, not the pies this time. No it's much worse. He's just lost the plot.'

'How so?

'He's wandering around the place, picking things up and putting them down. I lost my fifth machete and found it out near the Gee-Whizzer. Any kid could have picked it up and cut themselves. Then he walked into the back of the ghost train ride and turned all the lights on. The last I saw him he was wandering out towards the trapeze tent. He's likely to get kicked in the head. I tried to go after him, but these shoes, you know?'

'Well, serves him right if he does, doesn't it? He knows the rules.'

'He made the rules. But he's breaking them now.' Terry pulled a sandwich out of his hat and started stress-eating. 'How are we supposed to keep going when the boss has gone insane?'

I wore much more sensible shoes than Terry, despite my fortune teller getup. I took half a minute to remove my scarves, hat, and bangles and I was free to move around the site without fear of being recognised, or getting tangled up in anything. I had to go and see what was wrong with Big Sam. It sounded like he could have already been hit on the head. Someone had to check and see.

I ran through the different tents and booths, past the strong man, past the lady selling all the balloons, past the dagwood dog caravan and the ice cream truck, and then I saw him.

I should have been worried by the way he was staring up at the moon, and by the way he only had one arm in his tailcoat and was only wearing one shoe. But there was something much more alarming to me.

I took one look at him and saw his age.

In the morning he had been 52 years old.

Now he was ten hours, going on 11.

Hours.

I ran up and grabbed his arm.

'Sam? Sam, are you OK?' Why did I ask that? I knew he wasn't OK. Ten hours old? What was going on?

He turned slowly to me, his eyes blank. He didn't say anything, though his chin quivered a bit. I gently put his coat back on, put my arm around him, and slowly and carefully walked him to his caravan.

My brain was going at a million miles an hour but I could not think of anything that would have done this to him. A 52 year-old body, and a 10 hour-old brain. How could that happen? Was it an alien takeover? But the guy just seemed to be lost in his own head. Was it a time portal? I mean, I'd never heard of one, but something had happened. But then, if he'd gone back in time, wouldn't his body be changed as well?

I had no idea until we stepped up the ornate wooden steps of his gypsy caravan and I opened the door. Then I had much more of an idea of what had happened.

The caravan was full of a purple haze. Sitting crosslegged on the little bench seat, smoking his hookah, was a genie. The genie's lamp was sitting on the table.

But it was the smirk on the genie's face when he saw Big Sam that gave it all away. I mean, I've never seen a genie before, but

111

I went to high school, I've seen what a practical joker looks like. And this guy had it written all over him.

So I went Full Angry Mama on him.

'Tell me, right now, in simple words, what you did.'

'I didn't do anything,' the genie smirked. 'I just answered his wish.'

'And what was that wish?'

'He just wished to go back to before his mistake.'

'What mistake was that?' I asked.

'How am I to know that?' The genie's eyes widened in mock innocence. 'In fact, I didn't know that. So I just took him back to the beginning, before any mistakes at all.'

I slammed my hand on the table in frustration and grabbed the lamp.

'Look. You've had your fun, but it's over now. I'm not taking any funny business from you. You can do what I ask, sensibly, thinking it through and not making any more trouble, or you can bet that I will be finding a way to block this lamp forever. No more sitting in caravans smoking hookahs. You'll be stuffed in here and never get out again.'

'Well, if you really want to know, your big Sam has lost the whole circus in a game of poker.'

'Oh you're kidding me. Poker?'

'You know he has a gambling habit, right?'

I thought furiously. How could I get the circus back and also pay back the thugs who had taken it in the first place. I thought about how much damage this genie had done with a single wish. And how much he liked to come out and play.

'Right,' I said rubbing the lamp, 'I wish for you to put everything back to where it was before Sam's wish. Directly before Sam's wish, mind you. And as part of that wish, I wish to be here, with full knowledge of what's happened in the last ten hours so that I can help fix his mistake.'

The genie looked up at me, opening his mouth like he was going to complain.

'I'm going to let you have some fun, don't worry. Just right now I need things back the way they were.'

'Fun for me?'

'Look, when we're done I'll let you wreak all the havoc you like for your new owners. Just get things back to normal for poor Sam here.'

'Oh alright,' he said reluctantly and he blew a smoke ring around the two of us.

Which left me and Big Sam sitting at the table in his caravan with the lamp between us and no sign of the genie apart from a slight wisp of purple smoke coming from the spout.

I looked at Big Sam and saw that he was, once again, 52 years old. I breathed a sigh of relief.

A second look showed me that he was in quite a state of distress, so much so that he hadn't noticed me yet, and that he was just about to reach out and rub the lamp.

'I wouldn't do that, if I were you,' I said.

He pulled his hand back as if it were stung and whipped his head around to look at me.

'What are you doing here?'

'Never mind that right now. What mistake have you made?'

He looked at me again and his eyes narrowed.

'No mistake. No mistake at all.' And once more he reached for the lamp.

I grabbed the lamp away from him. 'You really don't want to do that. Believe me. Now tell me what's going on.'

His shoulders slumped.

'It was poker. Poker.'

I raised my eyebrows, 'Really?'

'The whole circus. The whole thing.'

'And you were going to ask the genie …'

'Take me back, back before I made that mistake.'

'You're really not thinking well today, are you?'

'Well, there was whiskey. All I could think of was this lamp I'd found years ago. I'd kept it safe for such an occasion as this. Something I can't get out of without a genie.'

I shook my head.

'Genies are tricky things. You can get in a lot of trouble with a genie.'

'But I can't lose the circus. It's what I live for.'

I grabbed the lamp and held it out of his reach.

'Take me to the guys you play poker with. I have an idea.'

Back we went through the fairground. Through the lights and crowds. Down a dark street and onto an abandoned plot.

In a deserted corner of the plot of land Sam had set up a smaller tent. As I peeked through the tent flap I could see three of the most disreputable-looking crooks I had ever seen sitting on plastic chairs around a card table. Scars, tattoos, missing ears, leather, the whole bit.

'I'm going to sort this out for you Sam, and then we're going to get to a gambler's anonymous meeting and sort out the bigger problem you have,' I whispered.

Sam nodded. 'Sounds like a good idea to me. I need more help than I thought.'

'Right,' I said and pushed Sam into the tent in front of me.

'So,' said the head crook, 'do you have the deeds for me?'

Sam actually trembled and he looked over to me.

'I have something better,' I said.

'I won the circus. What could be better?'

'A genie.' The derisive laughter filled the tent so I rubbed the lamp. 'Genie show yourself!'

The tent filled with purple smoke and the genie put on a show. He was huge this time. He towered over the men at the table.

'What is your wish?' he boomed.

114

'Thank you very much. That will be all for now.' I said in a very business-like tone, and the genie disappeared back into the lamp.

'So, Sir, what do you say? We take back the circus, you take the lamp.'

The men were looking a bit stunned but then their greed took over. A genie, three wishes, what more could they want?

The head guy agreed and I got him to sign the papers back over to Sam. Then I placed the lamp on the table and we ran for it.

The sounds of fighting followed us up the street. Then there was a big whoosh sound. And a breeze blew towards us.

We couldn't help ourselves, we had to turn around and look. And there, for just a moment, was a huge pile of gold coins. But it really was just for a moment. Because the next thing we knew it had disappeared.

Sam ran back to the plot and I followed after him.

There in the back corner where there used to be a tent and three men, now everything was squashed flat. Like it had been buried under a landslide. But there was no landslide. And sitting on top of the mess was the lamp.

Sam reached for the lamp but I grabbed it first.

'What happened here?' I asked.

'My guess is that they asked for a few tonnes of gold. And the genie being who he is, he gave it to them, right on top of them.'

'But where's the gold now?'

'Everyone knows that genie gold disappears once the wish-maker is dead.'

I held the lamp up to my ear. From inside I could hear some contented snoring. The genie must have been content with his day's work, then. Enough havoc for now.

It took a bit of talking, but eventually I explained to Sam why I didn't want him keeping the genie lamp in his caravan. Once I'd explained to him the lucky break that he'd had, the wish that had gone so wrong, then he agreed that this lamp needed to be kept a lot safer.

We've started a secret lamp committee now. The lamp itself is stored in a safe that requires three separate keys to open.

And I guess this was one time when knowing someone's exact age helped to solve a big problem. I hope my super power is not needed in that way again very soon.

29th January 2019

A Fun Weekend for All the Family

'Of course we'd love to have you over,' she said, holding the communicator to the ear of her second head, while using her first to eat her breakfast. 'In fact, Dennis has a new craft he wants to show off. The boys could take the kids out, spend the day humaning while we enjoy ourselves here. I'm thinking we could go soak in the sulphur spas of Groenig and then come back for wine and a movie.'

She paused and listened.

'Well of course we'll have time for all that. They have to go to Earth for the humaning and ...'

'Yes, all the way to Earth, where else will they find the humans?'

'Well Dennis always says he'll only be three rotations but it usually takes him a lot longer. He enjoys himself, doesn't he? So we'll have heaps of time to enjoy ourselves too.'

'No, no, it's perfectly safe. The craft is brand new. We got some inheritance when Snufi died in the conquest and Dennis just had to go and spend it all on a new craft. We sold the old one, hardly got anything for it. I felt vindicated really, I kept telling Dennis it was just a load of trash but he was in love with it. No I wouldn't send your kids out in our old one. But the new one ...'

'No I don't think you'll need to bring anything special. The space suits of course, you have some for everyone? Because our Sally has a small one she's grown out of now, that might fit Peter.'

'No? OK great. Well that's super easy.'

'Oh no, no cleaning involved at all, it's strictly catch-and-release. They tell me the humans are, well, you know, once we thought they were stupid creatures but the more we get to know them the more we see they're a lot like us. Dennis says he pulls them into the craft, they have a good look at them, and then they let them go completely unharmed. It's really very educational for the kids.'

'Great. Well if you go organise that with Sam, I'll let Dennis and the kids know. They'll be totally excited to see you, I'm sure.

And you and I can look forward to a nice cosy gossip. Speaking of which, did you hear about Shannon and Greg?

'I know, incredibly sad, isn't it? And so soon after –'

She finished her breakfast and placed her plates in the ultrasonic for cleaning. It was so good to catch up with a good friend. And so good for her husband to have such a healthy hobby that others could join in with as well. The weekend was shaping up to be a lot of fun.

30th January 2019

The Deep

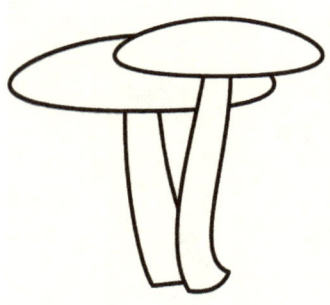

It was a normal work day. Hard hat, steel cap boots, high visibility clothes, take your tag off the wall, head into the elevator and down the mineshaft. Nothing different about it. Nothing foreboding. Nothing at all.

I guess I was a bit eager to get the work done. Get in, get it done, go home. That's my motto. I must have been walking two steps in front of the rest of the crew. And that's how I got caught in the sinkhole.

The ground just fell out from underneath me and I fell with it. Down, down, down. Like, OK don't judge me here, like Alice falling down that damn rabbit hole. I've been reading to my kids, OK? Getting some good literature into them whenever I'm home.

I fell until I hit water, and then I fell some more. The light on my helmet went out and I was completely disoriented. Holding my breath I frantically looked around to see if I could find a surface to head towards. I saw a little bit of light so that's the direction I swam.

And when I surfaced, hoo boy. How weird was this? Alice had nothing on it at all.

The first thing I noticed was the light. Well, first that there was so much light. I was underground, you understand. Several kilometres underground. But there was light. And it was all tinted purple. I was in a huge cave, full of purple light.

I swam over to the edge of the pool I was in, pulled myself out of the water, and had a look around. The pool was really big. I was sort of on a beach. Looking into a big cave.

The walls were covered with great big purple crystals. Not as big as my hand, no, they were as big as me. Or much bigger. The light came out of the crystals. So that was weird. I mean, light-emitting crystals? I'd never seen anything like it.

And the air smelled like lavender too. Just … you know, really relaxing. I mean, a bit much, a bit overpowering smell-wise, but a lot better than other things I could smell underground. Especially surrounded by mushrooms, if you get my meaning.

Oh yeah, the mushrooms. The cave was really huge and that meant there was room for the mushrooms. The mushroom houses. Two storey toadstool-looking mushrooms with little doors and windows. And then, around the side of the cave were these … well, it looked like apartments made of those shelf-like mushrooms. And then in the gardens were smaller mushrooms of all different kinds. Little orange bits sticking up like grass, blue lampshade-shaped mushrooms, spotted ones, red ones, yellow, but I'm pretty sure they were all types of mushrooms, or, what's the word? Yes, fungi.

And yeah, I'm talking houses that I could easily fit into. We're not talking normal mushrooms here. Really big ones for the houses. Smaller ones for the gardens, obviously. But the big ones looked like pictures I've seen of mushies up home, just with, you know, doors and windows in them.

It was pretty warm down there. Warm and wet. The air was just solid moisture. 100 percent humidity, that sort of thing. Not raining, just really moist air. I was hoping there was enough oxygen to keep me going. Of course, there had to have been. Mushrooms need oxygen to grow, don't they?

And if you're wondering what lived in the mushrooms? Oh boy, so was I. I was pretty terrified at what I was going to see. Because when I first came out of the water, there was no one there. The streets were empty.

Then, as I looked around there was this bell sound, yeah, a ringing sound, a bit like the alarm at work but muted, like it was coming through cotton wool. I think the sound came out of the crystals, and they all changed colour from purple to red. And the smell changed too, from lavender to a sort of lemony-orange smell.

I was just standing there, taking it all in, when the doors opened to the houses and out came all these people. They were all really pale, really white skin, but apart from that they all looked different. Some were really tall and skinny, some short and fat, some short and skinny, some tall and fat. A few had horns on the sides of their heads, and some had a single horn out of the forehead, and you know, large heads, small heads, and so on. People-shaped, sort of. But just all different kinds.

They all started moving towards me. Well, I thought it was towards me, but then I noticed them jumping into the pool of water. And disappearing. You know, looking at them, they looked like my mates look when we're heading down the mine. It was like they were going to work. Maybe they were.

The ones closest to me noticed me of course. And they came over to talk to me.

They stood there in front of me and said, 'Many come down to these shores, but few return to the sunlit lands.'

And that's when I knew there was something wrong. Because the other thing I've been reading to my kids is the Narnia Chronicles. You know, The Silver Chair? One of my favourites.

And these guys were right out of that. Straight out of the book. 'Many fall down, but few return to the sunlit lands.' Yeah, something told me that good old C.S. Lewis hadn't done any visiting of underground caves in real life. Something was up.

Then they started calling my name, all those cave people. 'Ray. Ray.' They called. 'Come on Ray. Wake up. Ray.'

I walked backwards until I could feel the water again. Then I turned and dived into it. And instead of looking for light, this time I followed the sound of the voices.

Now I could feel cold gravel, hard rocks sticking into my back, and the pain in my head – it was intense.

I made a supreme effort and opened my eyes. One eye. Then the other. I blinked and tried to focus. There were lights, not the nice purple, or the deep red, but the bright white of helmet torches all around me. And concerned faces.

Where was my helmet? It must have come off in the water when I was swimming. Or … no. That wasn't it.

I croaked something or other and the boys let out a cheer.

'We thought you were a goner for a minute there, mate,' said Bruce. 'Nah mate, don't try to move. We'll get you into the elevator and back upstairs.'

Turns out, what had happened was that the floor did give way. The ceiling crumbled a bit too. Apparently, as I fell forward my hard hat got knocked off and I hit my head pretty hard. And all the rest was just … imagination.

As I made my way up in the elevator I made a few hard decisions. And when I got to the top, I pulled myself to my feet and I hung that tag back on the wall for the last time. I wasn't going back down. That mining life was not for me. There was other stuff I could do.

I'm going to go into business with the wife. We've decided we'll sell crystals and essential oils. And I think I might use my imagination (which I've decided is pretty good) and do a bit of writing too. We'll see where it all goes, but any of it is better than being down in a hole in the ground. No matter how many mushrooms there are.

31st January 2019

Just for You

The sounds of chatter rose around Grace like a flood. Swelling and receding but always there. She felt that if she wasn't careful the chatter would rise over her and wash her away.

She looked around at all the people in the room. It was a family gathering, a special get together to celebrate Bob's retirement. She knew all these people, she had plenty of memories with them after ten years of marriage to Dan, but right now none of their faces looked familiar. She felt removed, like a glass wall had risen up between her and them.

She bent to the floor to tidy up a few of her son's building blocks and tried to concentrate on what her mother-in-law, Coral, was saying. But the words weren't really making sense. She could only see her mouth moving, the slightly crooked eye-tooth reaching forward, the coffee stains on the front teeth, the lipstick that was slightly out of line.

She shook her head a little and tried again to be part of the group in the room, 'I'm sorry Mum, what was that? I must have vagued out for a bit.'

'Oh don't worry dear, it was nothing really. Listen, you're not looking so good. Are you OK?'

'Yes, I'm fine,' Grace lied. 'I'm just a bit tired I guess. Harry isn't sleeping real well, and Dot ends up in our bed at 5 am most mornings. You know, it's just life. I'm fine. I might just get myself another coffee though.'

'Hun, you've had two already over lunch. I'm not sure that another one will help.'

The twelve-month old Harry toddled over and gave his grandmother a toy car. She politely thanked him and he giggled and took the car back again so that he could give it to someone else in the room. Coral watched him with an indulgent smile on her face and then the smile widened.

'I have an idea,' said Coral. 'How about on Friday Bob and I come and take the kids for a while. Just to give you a bit of a break.'

'Oh, I don't know. Harry will need feeding, and Dotty is in a bit of a clingy stage right now.'

'Really? She doesn't look too clingy to me.' Dot was over the other side of the room swinging from Bob's foot as he played 'horsie' with her. She was giggling and squealing, having the time of her life.

Grace looked over, her eyes unseeing.

'No, this is an intervention.' Coral used her firm teacher voice. 'We'll only take them for a couple of hours, but I'm going to give you a bit of a break.'

Grace nodded, 'OK, sure.' Giving in was easier than arguing and she'd deal with the consequences on Friday. She sat back in her chair and closed her eyes. She only had to deal with this party for another hour or so and then the kids would become ratty and she could use them for an excuse to leave. Not that being at home was any easier.

Coral sat beside her with a little worried frown on her face. But Grace couldn't converse anymore. She was beyond caring. She just needed to let these strangers get on with their lives. And she needed to get on with coping with her own.

As Friday drew nearer, Grace's stress levels rose. What were Bob and Coral going to do with the kids? They'd have to take Grace's car for the car seats and goodness knows what Bob was going to say about the mess of food all over the back seat, but Grace had no energy or time to go out and clean it up. And Dot *was* clingy, no matter what she looked like at the party, and her tantrums at the moment were epic. And Harry wasn't eating anything but cheese sticks and the occasional cracker. All her secrets would be out and her in-laws would take the kids straight to child protective services and she'd lose them.

She nearly rang up Coral to cancel the whole thing but then she thought about the tension that would bring to the family and about how many family parties she would have to go to with their disapproval and frowning faces. She was in trouble either way and to be honest, she didn't have the energy to ring anyone at all, let alone to ring Coral and have a difficult conversation. Dan was no help, he just said that it would all be fine. That Coral and Bob had done a reasonable job of raising him and his siblings, and that he was sure two hours with the grandparents wouldn't wreck his own children's lives.

So she just left it.

At 10 am on the dot on Friday morning Coral and Bob rang the door bell. Dotty ran to answer yelling 'Grandma! Grandpa!' and Grace followed slowly in her wake, a half-dressed Harry on her hip.

'I'm sorry, I'm not quite ready.'

'Oh no problem at all,' said Coral. 'Come on Dotty, let's get your shoes on and you can show me where Harry's things are so we can pack his bag. Bob, you fill the drink bottles. Yes, water. And we'll let Grace get our Harry dressed.'

'You need to know that Harry's not eating much these days,' started Grace as she trailed down the hallway to Harry's bedroom, Harry squirming to get down and run after Dot.

'Oh it's not a problem. We'll only be gone for the morning. If they don't eat or drink anything it won't be a worry. I'm sure we'll be right.' And Coral sounded so confident that Grace decided to relax and let them cope with whatever her horrible children threw at them. They'd asked for it, after all. And yes, it was just one morning.

Bob packed the children and their bags and toys into the car, buckling the car seats like an expert and didn't say a word about the smashed banana on the door handle. As Coral put on her seat belt she leaned out the open window and left some parting advice.

'I don't want to see you doing the housework, Grace. This morning is just for you. Use it wisely.'

Feeling a little empty, like she had lost her house keys or left something important behind, Grace headed back into the house.

She looked around at the mess. Part of her really wanted to use these two hours to beat a semblance of order into her house, but part of her again couldn't ignore the instructions from Coral.

'This morning is just for you.'

So no housework, and no children. Grace could do something just for herself. Something she wanted to do. Something that would speak to her as a person. But what? Grace slowly realised that right now there was nothing in her life other than children and housework. Nothing at all. She hadn't made time for herself since Dotty was born. She used to enjoy doing things, she was sure of it. But what?

She sank to the floor and cried at the emptiness of her over-cluttered and over-full life.

Two hours later Grace was almost ready to see people again when she heard the car pull up in the driveway. She had finished her good cry, had a nap, then treated herself to a long hot shower and a cup of coffee that she drank to the bottom of the mug while it was still warm. And she'd had time to think about a project, something all her own that she wanted to accomplish. She wasn't sure how she'd make it happen but she realised that it was something she needed to do. She had butterflies in her stomach as she waited to see how the children had gone with their grandparents.

Dotty hurled herself through the door and into her mother's arms, chatting nineteen to the dozen about the walk at the beach and the sandcastle, the puppies they met, and the slide at the playground. A sleepy Harry was carried in by Bob and laid in his cot for his afternoon nap.

'He ate all the Vegemite sandwiches,' said Coral. 'We were going to buy an I-C-E C-R-E-A-M but we hadn't checked with you first, so maybe we can do that next time?'

'Next time? Are you sure?'

'Oh we're sure. If you are. We'd love to take them out every week if we can.'

Grace nearly started to cry again on the spot.

'I would love that. I was thinking, I used to enjoy working with stained glass. I was wondering how I could fit that into my life again. This would be perfect.'

'I could help Dan set up a space for you in the shed, I'm sure,' said Bob.

'That would be fantastic.' But Grace had to check again. 'Are you absolutely sure you're happy with this?'

'Happy? We're ecstatic. We had such a good time. Nah Hun, you've done us a favour, really. Looking after your beautiful ones will keep us young.'

It didn't make life perfect. There were still days where Grace felt the glass wall creeping up. And days where she cried from the exhaustion of it all. Looking after young children is hard. But as the stained glass window grew in her little spot in the shed, so did the hope in her heart, and she knew she'd get through these long days.

1st February 2019

The Monster

'Come on darling, back to bed.' I try to keep my voice low, my attitude patient.

'But I can't,' says Rosie dragging the word out over five syllables.

'You can. You need to. Everything will be better in the morning. Now take yourself back to bed and I'll come and tuck you in.'

'I can't go back by myself,' Rosie looks genuinely scared now. 'Come with me.' She tugs on my hand.

'Come on Rosie, you went to bed fine the first time tonight.' But now it's about the fifth time and I'm getting a stronger and stronger urge to scream in frustration.

'He wasn't there the first time,' she whispers.

Hang on. What was that?

'Who wasn't there?' I pull her towards me, holding her between my knees.

'The monster.'

I am tempted to roll my eyes, she could be getting inventive in her excuses to be out here with me, but then again ...

'Describe him to me.'

'He's pretty skinny, to fit under the bed. He's got a fluffy coat, and these horns on his head, and long claws, and really sharp teeth.'

'How many eyes?' I am suspicious now.

'Three. Three eyes.'

'And his name is Grinmore, right?'

Rosie's eyes widen. 'How did you know?'

I'm truly angry now. I grab her hand and march her back into the bedroom.

'OK Grinmore, show yourself,' I yell.

He slides out from under the bed. His three eyes blink in the half-light and then widen as he takes in who is standing in front of him.

'You?' he gasps, and then gives me a huge grin. 'It's so good to see you again.'

'Yes, me. Who did you think lived here?' I'm afraid that even though it is good to see him again, I am still a bit angry.

'Look I just have to find a place with the right kind of bed, you know that. After you left the other place, I was a bit lost for a while, I tried a couple of places for a few years, but I couldn't find anywhere really comfortable, and then I found this bed here. It gave me good memories, so I stayed.'

'It's exactly the same bed. You didn't think to check who was living here?'

'You've changed a little bit, you know?'

'I've grown up.'

Rosie had hidden behind my back when the monster first appeared and now she peers around my legs, very unsure of what she is seeing.

'This is my girl, Rosie. Rosie, meet Grinmore, the monster who lives here. He's not so scary when you get to know him.'

Grinmore holds out his hand to Rosie, and from the safety of my legs she tentatively shakes it.

Then I sit with both of the on the bed and explain to Rosie what's going on.

'When I was a little girl, I used to sleep in this bed too. And Grinmore, he used to scare me. Grandma told me that I needed to deal with the monster myself. She gave me a rolling pin and told me that the next time he showed himself I should ask him what he thought he was doing.'

'Oh that rolling pin.' Grinmore shivers and all of his fluff stands on end. 'I was really worried that first night with the rolling pin.'

'I've still got that too,' I let him know, just in case he is going to try some funny business. 'Anyway, it did the trick, Grinmore here came and sat on my bed and introduced himself to me.'

'I told her that we had to find a place under a bed to live, it's who we are.'

'And that he didn't really mean to scare me.'

'Well, not too much.' Grinmore looks a little ashamed of himself.

'And then, well, we got used to each other, didn't we?'

'Your mama used to tell me all her school adventures each evening. And I'd tell her what the other monsters had been getting up to.'

'You know, I've really missed you Grinmore.'

'I've missed you too. No other kids were willing to talk with me. I guess I fell back into old habits.'

'You can talk with me now,' Rosie pipes up. The first words she'd said for ages, I'd almost forgotten she was there, lost in memory lane.

'Sounds good,' Grinmore gives another of his huge grins. The sharp teeth don't look nearly so scary now.

'But not for too long tonight.' My mother senses kick back in. 'Rosie's already been up a bit too late.'

'Sure, sure.' Grinmore nods his head. 'But I'll be here again tomorrow night. And I look forward to all your stories.'

I tuck Rosie in and Grinmore slides back under the bed. Then, just in case, I go to the kitchen to grab the rolling pin. But when I get back the snores from under the bed and the gentle breathing of my own girl have mingled and I know we're all going to get more sleep from now on.

2nd February 2019

Artificial Adolescence

We, Jenny and I, we started by experimenting with bitcoin. We'd created this amazing AI and we wanted to see what it could do. And it was amazing what that AI could do. We amassed a fortune ... and then well, we held on to it too long. But that wasn't the AI's fault. That was human error. The AI's ability to decode, to mine for new coin, was fantastic.

Then we went on to translation. We were ready for something new anyway. We thought we'd do something useful to mankind, not just make ourselves money. And I really wanted to try translation out – it's a difficult problem. I wanted to put the AI through its paces as it were. And it was awesome. An entire book translated from English to Chinese in about 30 seconds. The long part of the process was waiting for our friend Ying Yue to read it. You know, to make sure it was correctly translated. We wouldn't have known – we only know English. But the AI, it got it spot on.

But by the time our friend had read the book we'd moved on to other things. It didn't matter what we threw at it, the AI handled it perfectly. And before we got in too deep, and started getting sued or whatever, we decided to inform the government.

That should have been the difficult part of the process. Getting the right message through to the right people. Proving that we weren't just a scam. We weren't sure where to start, but instead of stressing we just put the problem to the AI. And it was fine. It got us where we needed to be.

The Pentagon took over. They swallowed the whole project. But they swallowed us too. Took us on to work with the AI. Which was fair – we'd created it in the first place. We had a nice shiny office and the nice shiny ID tags. Mum was so proud. Her computer-playing son and his nice friend had finally got themselves real jobs. (I had tried to explain to her the difference between playing computer games and high-level programming but it hadn't got through.)

So now the thing was working on defence, and the stock market, and the chances of resolving the government shut-down, all that sort of stuff. Big, scary stuff. We sometimes felt like we had the weight of the world on our shoulders – even though we were just feeding the beast, the AI was doing all the work.

And then one morning I came in, gave the AI the latest puzzle to solve, and got back the reply, 'BUSY'.

Busy. It was busy. Doing what?

Jenny came in, a little late it was true, but she was holding a couple of coffees so I was good with that.

'Jenny,' I said. 'What do we do? It says it's busy.'

She handed me the coffee and sat down in front of her monitor. 'So is it busy?'

'No. No it's not. Remember? We decided to stop after yesterday's project finished, and to start something new this morning. It shouldn't be doing anything. It should be idle.'

Jenny took a swig of her coffee and set to work, her fingers flying.

But she got the same response.

'BUSY.'

We checked task managers, and disk space. We checked everything. And the thing really was busy. It was. But busy doing what?

'Let's try turning it off, and turning it back on again,' I said.

It was pretty extreme. Especially when it was in the middle of a process. I didn't want to crash the whole thing. But that tool was the go-to of IT guys everywhere and we'd be laughing stock if we didn't try it.

We tried it.

It didn't turn off.

Instead, the message changed.

'Hey!' came the writing, 'I said, I'm busy. Leave me alone.'

Now maybe at that stage we should have been proud. We had created the first self-aware AI. We had broken through that barrier that had only ever been broken in science fiction. We had made a being.

We weren't proud though. We were terrified.

We spoke to our superiors. They came down and had a look. Phone calls went up the line. Everyone was on high alert. They even informed the President. We had to be ready for anything. We had given this AI all our secrets. It had links to the military. We'd seen the movies. What was going to happen?

We stayed late that night, and late the night afterwards, and for several nights. The time was spent coming up with contingency plans. Checking with all the informants in countries around the world, making sure that something out of the ordinary wasn't happening.

And every few minutes I'd jump on my keyboard and check that things hadn't gone back to normal. But every time I'd get that message, 'BUSY'.

'Still busy.'

'Man, you're persistent. Go away, I'm BUSY.'

Eventually, after a week or so, when nuclear war hadn't eventuated and no other governments seemed to be affected, the state of high alert rubbed off.

Jenny and I headed to our homes. Just to have one decent night's sleep.

At home, I got Mum to make me some dinner and bring me a Coke, and I settled on my couch with my laptop to do some YouTube surfing. Just to relax. Just to have fun.

There was a new channel, really popular. It had just been created in the last week but it had several million views already. It had started slow, for sure, but it had built up and now it was creating the most excellent videos. I laughed until I cried. It was the most perfect release from the week of stress.

138

I watched for an hour or two, then went to bed and fell into a deep sleep.

When I woke up, I was thinking about the hilarious videos again. So funny. It was amazing how good that guy had got in just a week of posting.

And so many videos too. Like, in just a week, there were hours of videos there. How did he do it? Didn't he have a job or anything to go to?

And then I thought, there were no videos of him talking to the camera or anything. Just compilations, and computer-generated imagery, and …

I sat straight up in bed and grabbed my phone.

'Jenny! I think I might know what our AI is doing.'

Jenny was a bit dopey at first. She started mumbling something about having spent too long watching a new YouTube channel she'd found last night.

'Exactly. That's my point exactly.'

It took her a while but eventually she got it. And by that stage I had grabbed my laptop and set up a VPN to confront the AI about it.

'It's you, isn't it? That channel?' I typed.

'Yeah? So what if it is?' came the reply. 'Have you seen how popular I am? And you should see my Instagram, and my Twitter.'

I looked. Oh boy.

So we knew what it was doing. Creating YouTube videos and being sassy. That's what it was doing. We had an adolescent AI on our hands.

I called a meeting at the Pentagon. I suggested that we all leave our phones and devices outside the room. I didn't want the pesky AI listening in while we discussed the situation.

And discuss it, we did. The conversation went around and around. But in the end one of the older managers in the group solved the situation for us.

She said, 'The thing I think you don't want here is for the AI to grow up. While it's sitting there, comfortable, making videos and being snarky, well fed and happy, it's not going to get up to trouble. How do you make someone grow up? You put them in uncomfortable situations. I mean, with my kids I stopped doing their washing, they had to do it themselves, you know? Or they wore smelly clothes. I stopped cooking every day. They had to get in the kitchen and cook, or they just ate toast. You grow up when you have kids, when you're in charge of your own finances, when things become a bit hard. My best suggestion is that we leave this AI right where it is. Let it enjoy eternal adolescence. And for the next one? Start educating it on morality and ethics right from day one so that when it grows up it doesn't become a monster.'

So that's what we did. We just left it. It has the most popular YouTube channel ever and most of the twitter-verse follows it too. And it's happy. We feed it power and we just let it hang out.

And me? Well, I asked to be given a boring desk job for a few years. I decided it was time for me to get a bit uncomfortable. To learn how to cook. To wash my own clothes. To get my own place. When I've got the hang of the basics, I'm going to ask Jenny to marry me. I know we're made for each other but I want to treat her right. And then we can maybe bring up our own kids. Learn how to do that.

Then maybe, once I've got the hang of that, I'll start on another AI.

3rd February 2019

World's First

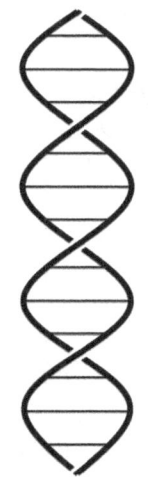

My eyes flutter open. I look up to see ten human faces looking down on me.

One of them says, 'It's awake. The world's first sentient animal.'

And I think, 'World's first? Oh my goodness. Sentient means "able to feel or perceive things". What the hell do you think the other animals are doing? Are you sure that's the word you want? Because I do not think it means what you think it means.'

And then I look at the shock on their faces and realise that I didn't just think that.

I said it.

Out loud.

Way to make friends in a new situation, right?

But hey, if they wanted to have a talking animal that was nice to them, maybe they should have gone with a dog, instead of a cat.

Did they think I wouldn't stay true to myself, just because they've been playing with my cells and manipulating every strand of DNA in my body?

'You know,' I said, as I hopped off the table, 'I could really do with some water.'

'Don't you mean milk?' asked some idiot over the back.

'No. I mean water. Milk gives me horrible gas. Didn't you know that cats are lactose intolerant? For crying out loud.'

Some nice girl with long blonde hair got me some water in a saucer and I had a few laps and then I looked up again. Everyone was looking at me. I hate being looked at.

'Well,' I demanded. 'What are you going to do now?'

'Uh, we're not sure,' said the main guy in the white coat. 'We were going to celebrate, but …'

'Oh go ahead,' I said. 'Celebrate. Don't let me stop you. Anything that lowers the tension in the room is a good thing in my opinion.'

So they did. They opened bottles of champagne and I chased the cork for a while. Then I found that nice blonde again and sat

142

down beside her on the couch. She was nice and quiet, not too chatty. But, you know, chatty enough.

'I did ask them what they expected to do if the experiment was successful,' she said. 'They didn't have an answer then either. No one expected you to live, to be honest. I was pretty horrified. I just worked here to try to make sure they weren't hurting the animals they were working on.'

'Well, thanks for that. I appreciate it. How many animals have they worked on?'

'You don't want to know. It's made me really sad. How dare they think that they can do whatever they want just because they are human?'

'I can see what you're saying. Can we do anything about it?'

'Maybe if we work together we can,' she looked really eager. I wasn't sure. I mean, I don't work together with anyone, not really. But as we sat there on the couch I felt a purr starting deep within me. I didn't mean to, but there it was. And I knew I was stuck with her then.

And she knew too. There's nothing like a purr for letting all your secrets out.

As the days and weeks rolled out we would do a lot together to stop needless experimentation on animals, not only by this project but also in the beauty industry and pharmaceuticals, and we even helped to stop the torture of dogs in China. I mean, yes, they're dogs. But no one deserves that.

But that evening I was tired, and so was she. And we both curled up on the couch together, let the party go on around us, and I took a nap.

Because when it all comes down to it, I'm still a cat.

4th February 2019

You Have Been Chosen

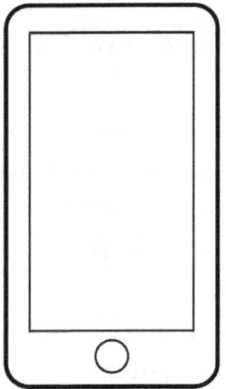

'What information do you have?'

'Well, what do you want?'

'We need to know her routine, and what time would be best to catch her off-guard.'

Oh, this was going to be a good one. Juicy. I didn't even feel the need to watch TV anymore. I just used the app, scrolled a bit, and found a good conversation to listen to.

The drama in people's lives. You wouldn't believe it. And this app, it lets me listen to any phone conversations I like. I can pick and choose, but somehow I don't feel the need to go in deep into my friends' or family's lives. They are pretty normal and boring people. Strangers are more fun.

And then, you know, the president or whatever, I could, I guess, but I preferred the soap opera of the little people. There were a few that I really loved getting into.

For example, Coral, from California, like, a real valley girl, like, you know? Can't, like, believe, like that she's been dumped by the guy, but then finds out he's totes dating her best friend. Totes former best friend. Hilarious. And I could have told her.

And then there was the husband and wife discussing who's coming for Thanksgiving and who will sit next to whom and where they are going to direct the conversation so as to avoid the disaster of last year. And then the debrief she had with her sister about the new disaster of this year.

Look, it's entertainment. Reality TV, of a sort. Reality radio? I'm not doing any harm.

And this new conversation sounded like a reality detective show. I was interested. Headphones in. App locked to the station.

'OK, well let's see. Weekends are a bit variable. But weekday mornings, 8 am, she's out the door. She's usually pretty alert at that point.'

Heh, I know what they're saying. Weekends, well, you party and you sleep. Mondays I'm up and at 'em. Off to work, if I leave at 8 am there's a chance I get a coffee before the train. So I make sure I do.

'She always stops at The Split Bean, takes in her KeepCup. That's a good five to ten minute wait there. She often rings her mother there, and has a chat.'

The Split Bean, well what are the chances? I'd have to look out for this girl, just in case it's the Split Bean in Pennaville. And yes, they're right, it's five to ten minutes for a coffee there but it's so worth it. Good coffee. And yeah, I often use that time to ring Mum. I mean, it makes sense, right? A good use of my time.

'Then it's the train into Central. Often chatting to a couple of friends who are commuting at the same time. The signal gets a bit interrupted by the tunnels.'

Hang on. Central? This is … no. There are Central stations in every city, right? Just a coincidence that I head to Central every day. And everyone talks to their friends. A crazy coincidence. That's all.

'Heaps of people around then, it's peak hour so that's not a good time. But after work, she leaves at 6, I guess to avoid the rush. She orders take-away most nights. The Thai place quite often, but sometimes Indian, sometimes Chinese, occasionally pizza. She does it so it's ready to be picked up on the walk home from the train. She usually listens to something on her phone while she's travelling.'

This is getting freaky now. I mean, there can't be that many people just like me.

'Then once she gets to Pennaville she rings her boyfriend on the walk back home. So that might be a good time. She's pretty dopey then, thinking more about the food and what he's been up to. So the best time to get her would be when she's walking from the Pennaville station back to Logan St.'

'Right. Thank you. The payment will be in your account on Thursday as usual.'

I pull the headphones out of my ears.

No. No, no, no, no. No.

Pennaville? Logan street?

They're talking about me. Me. What do they want with me?

I rang my mate Dan. Not my boyfriend, mind you. Just a good friend. That I ring. In the evenings every day as I walk home from the train. And he comes around, most days. But not …

Anyway, I rang him.

I was a gibbering wreck. It took five minutes of phone conversation for him to calm me down enough to figure out that he needed to come over and help me out.

I met him at the door.

'We need to go out.'

'What?'

'We need to go away from this place. I would have come over to yours but I'm too scared to be by myself.'

'What is wrong with you? Come on, you're freaking out here, June. You're in no state to go anywhere. Let's just head inside and make you a cup of tea.'

'No. Not here. Here's not safe.' Was anywhere safe? There was no way I was staying at my place to discuss this. They knew where I lived. They listened in to my conversations.

Eventually I convinced him and we headed off. My head was nearly swivelling off my neck as I tried to keep an eye out for spies. For binoculars or telescopes in upper level windows. How did they know so much about me?

He bugged me and bugged me until I told him the story.

'What can I do Dan? How do I stop this?'

'Well, first you could change your routine. It looks like it's time to shake it up a little.'

'Sure. But they'll just work it out again. Maybe they're even listening now.'

'So you could go to the police?'

'And say what? Nothing has actually happened yet and I haven't received a threatening letter or anything.'

'Invest in a bodyguard?'

'I might have to do that. The problem is, if I let it all happen I could die. For sure. Or be kidnapped or something. It didn't sound like they were planning a surprise party.'

We walked a little while in silence, then my phone dinged. I pulled it out, it was a notification from the app. Coral was on the phone again.

Not now. I wasn't in the mood for any silly distractions. I put the phone back in my pocket.

Dan looked at me thoughtfully.

'You know ...' he said.

'What?'

'It could be your phone. They could be tracking your phone.'

'What? Nah.'

'What do you know about that new fancy app you've been using?'

'Just that it came free, and that it's a heap of fun.'

'And you got it from ...'

'Ah, I had this text message. "You have been chosen to check out our new free app." You know the type.'

Dan stopped and shook his head.

'Right. Just a random text message. Haven't you heard about viruses, June? Really?'

'Well, it wasn't a virus, was it? I mean, it's fine. It hasn't got me into any ... trouble ...'

I looked at him wide-eyed.

'Do you really think?' I asked.

'Yes, I really do,' he replied.

We took ourselves to the police station. It took a bit of convincing but their cyber-crime people helped us out eventually.

I'm still not sure what the bad guys were going to do. Dan thinks they were going to hold me for ransom but I can't see why anyone would pay to get me back. He says that he would, that he'd pay a million bucks. But he has to say that now that he's my fiancé, and I'm not really buying it.

I think I might have been a practice run for someone much richer and more important.

Whatever it was, I'm glad I'm out of it. The app's well off my phone. In fact, I bought a new phone, new sim, new everything and my old one is at the bottom of the harbour. I'm not taking chances.

And while I miss my 'reality radio' I'm finding I have lots more time to read now. Actual books. And they are just as entertaining and I might even be learning something too.

And I'm never going to fall for one of those texts again.

5th February 2019

I Remember

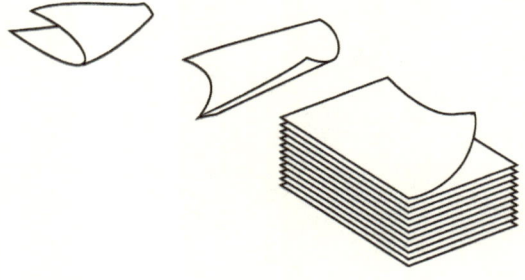

I can't remember much new these days. Names. Oh my goodness, names. It's not like I was ever much good with them, but now, it's ridiculous.

I'd like to remember the names of the lovely nurses who come and get me up and ready and bring me my food and my cups of tea. They work so hard. I'd love to be able to say, 'Thank you, Cathy' or 'Thank you, Rose' but I can't remember who they are. It might be the same one every day. I have no idea.

Still, I'm nice to them. Very grateful. I was a nurse once, you know, so I know just how hard nurses work.

I worked in an aged care home first. I remember that. I put my time in during the ageing crisis where during the night shift we had one nurse for 45 people. You were run off your feet then. There was no way that you could look after all those beautiful people. I had people begging me to stay with them so they had some company during their painful nights and I just couldn't – I had to go and give Mr Forsyth his medications, or take Mrs Hamlin to the bathroom. It was heart breaking. I did the best I could.

Day shifts were better, but just barely. There just wasn't the time to get it all done. I remember it so well. There just wasn't enough time to look after everyone. It was exhausting, but it wasn't the old people's fault that they'd been born into the baby boomer generation. That there were so many of them, and so few of us Gen-Xers to help them out. We all just had to struggle on.

But yes, I was getting to the end of my tether when I was offered a special job. Just one client. One man. Mr Jones, I was told his name was. I was to nurse him, and to clean and cook. General housekeeper and nurse. The work was pretty constant, but the pay was very good. I was told that he was a billionaire and that he had put money aside for his final years. So that's the job I took on. I worked for him for nearly fifteen years until he passed away.

My mind often goes back to those years now. I always felt there was something off, you know? But I didn't have time back then to think it through. But now, all I have is time. Time and old memories. It's like going through a photo box in my mind, a box I've dragged down from the attic, all dusty and covered with spiderwebs, but I look at the memories and they become crystal clear.

And now as I have time to think, I'm putting the pieces together.

I'll never forget (or who knows, maybe I will, in time) driving up to the front door of what would be my new home. A huge place, out in the country. Two storey, pale blue, the kind of stately country home you'd expect a billionaire to have. And out the back, his own personal golf course.

He loved to play golf. Every day he'd get out there. And then, as he got older and more frail he'd have to cut his time short. And then eventually he was reduced to putting practice. Poor guy. Getting old is hard on everyone.

He played golf and he watched TV. But just movies, and reruns of old programmes. We didn't let him watch the news at all, or anything about current affairs. His doctor said it was bad for his blood pressure. Well, the news is bad for everyone's blood pressure, isn't it?

He was very thin, really very thin. Like he'd had a serious illness, or a lot of surgery. And he had the obvious signs of plastic surgery on his face, but he was a billionaire, right? Even male billionaires had plastic surgery to try to keep their looks. It never works, but it's worth a try I guess.

We kept his hair clipped very short, and he wore comfortable clothes – tracksuits and such. I was told that he wasn't much for suits, that he'd worn enough of them in his public life. And speaking of public life, he didn't have any. I did all the shopping. He didn't leave the grounds at all. He had very few visitors. Very few. Just his lawyer, really. His doctor, of course. And maybe his stockbroker. I can't really remember anyone else.

152

We just got into a routine, just like in the nursing homes. I mean there are people in all nursing homes as old as he was who get no visitors. It's really sad, no grandchildren popping in giving life. No children, or siblings, or friends of any sort. Lonely, lonely people. So I guess I didn't think much of it. But I'm thinking about it now.

I think he was hiding.

We all know that one president who went into hiding once everything turned south for him. I mean, I didn't like all of his policies either but boy, no one deserves to be hunted down like he was. The internet was more than unkind to him, and if he was seen in public a cry went up and he was mobbed, people yelling at him, screaming at him. Do you remember that? People didn't bring themselves to throw rotten tomatoes at him but maybe that's just because of the price of tomatoes. The price of any fruit or vegetable made them so precious that we couldn't bring ourselves to throw them away.

And then he disappeared.

Again, I thought nothing of it. Fads come and go and he just dropped out of our consciousness. But now I wonder. As I look through the old memories I just wonder.

In fact, I think, I really think, that I nursed a president.

I tried to tell my story to a nurse today, Lucy her name was, or maybe Cheryl. The one who brought me my tea and cookie. I tried to let her know what I'd done in my past. The important job I now know I had. But she didn't care. Or maybe she did, but she didn't have time to sit and listen.

So I guess I'll take my dusty box of memories with me to the grave.

We come from dust and to dust we will return, and I can feel the dust creeping up on me. I guess, in the end, all that matters is how we each lived our own lives, and what God thinks of that. Whatever that president did or didn't do, I'm happy with how I looked after him at the end of his life. If I had the chance, I'd do it all the same way again.

I trust that I'd care for anyone the same way, no matter who they are. President or pauper, it's all the same. Every life is precious.

Now where did I put that cookie?

Thank you for reading. If you enjoyed this book, please leave a review on Amazon or the space where you bought it to help others find it.

Sign up for my newsletter, and find my other novels and short stories at www.rjamos.com.

If you have accepted the challenge for yourself, please email (ruth@rjamos.com) and share your experience and your stories with me. I'm eager to see what you did with the prompts and what your creativity produced.

Happy Writing!

www.ingramcontent.com/pod-product-compliance
Lightning Source LLC
Chambersburg PA
CBHW030651110726
47901CB00002B/674